The Hardy Boys Mystery Stories

Available from MINSTREL Books

116

The HARDY BOYS®

ROCK 'N' ROLL RENEGADES

FRANKLIN W. DIXON

A MINSTREL BOOK

PUBLISHED BY POCKET BOOKS

New York   London   Toronto   Sydney   Tokyo   Singapore

A MINSTREL PAPERBACK *ORIGINAL*

A Minstrel Book published by
POCKET BOOKS, a division of Simon & Schuster Inc.
1230 Avenue of the Americas, New York, NY 10020

Copyright © 1992 by Simon & Schuster Inc.
Front cover illustration by Daniel Horne
Produced by Mega-Books of New York, Inc.

ISBN: 0-671-73063-0

First Minstrel Books printing October 1992

10 9 8 7 6 5 4 3 2 1

THE HARDY BOYS MYSTERY STORIES is a trademark of Simon & Schuster Inc.

THE HARDY BOYS, A MINSTREL BOOK, and colophon are registered trademarks of Simon & Schuster Inc.

Printed in the U.S.A.

Contents

ROCK 'N' ROLL
RENEGADES

1 The Voice from Nowhere

"This is your favorite deejay and mine, Joltin' Joe Hardy, spinning the twin turntables and bringing home all the hottest hits! It's three o'clock in the afternoon, and you're listening to WBBX, the Big B in Bayport, where you can win a hundred dollars each time we play the secret hit of the day."

Muscular seventeen-year-old Joe Hardy leaned over the electronic console in front of him, pressed a button to turn off the microphone, and turned a couple of knobs. Then he removed a set of headphones from his blond head and scooted backward in his swivel chair. Rock music blared down from a speaker mounted on the rear wall of the tiny room where he sat.

"What twin turntables?" asked Joe's husky friend

1

Chet Morton, who was standing behind Joe's chair. "All I see you playing is CDs."

"I heard a disc jockey say that when I was a kid, and I thought it sounded neat," Joe replied. "We still use the turntables for the music that's not out on CD," he explained, pointing to the equipment at the side of the room.

"Stations that play the golden oldies probably still use records," said Joe's dark-haired older brother, Frank Hardy. "And college radio stations use records, too, if they don't have the money to replace them with CDs," Frank added.

"Yeah," Joe said. "Now I've got to pick out the CDs I'm going to play on tomorrow's program."

He stood and walked to a wooden shelf unit next to the console, where dozens of CDs were lined up in their clear plastic cases. As he thumbed through the wide selection of titles, he thought about how excited he was to have gotten this summer job as a disc jockey at his favorite radio station. Four weeks earlier he had been a summer intern in the station's advertising department. Then one of the regular announcers had been unexpectedly forced to leave the station. Joe had filled in for him, and the station manager was so pleased with Joe's work that he had given him his own show after school. It was only temporary, until the station manager could find a full-time replacement, but so far Joe was having a ball.

"Speaking of golden oldies," Joe said, pulling a CD from a stack. "Here's 'Truckin'' by the Grateful

2

Dead. According to the label, the cut is five minutes and nine seconds long, so I'll have time to run a PSA and still backtime the song up to the half-hour news."

"Huh?" Chet said, furrowing his brow.

"I knew it," Frank said with a laugh. "No sooner does my kid brother get a job talking on the radio than he forgets how to speak English."

Joe settled back into the swivel chair and pulled the headset over his ears. He gave his brother and Chet a dirty look. "A PSA is a public service announcement. They're produced by nonprofit groups, and we play them for free. Backtiming means timing a record so that it will end at exactly the time you want it to, usually when the half-hour news comes on. Now, keep it down, you guys. When I invited you to spend the afternoon at the station, you promised you wouldn't do anything that would get you—or me—kicked out of the studio."

"And we won't," Frank agreed. "Will we, Chet?"

"No way," Chet said.

Joe plugged the CD into a small disc player above the console, then swiveled a microphone mounted on a mechanical arm until it was barely more than an inch away from his mouth. He threw a switch on the console and began to speak.

"It's three twenty-three in the afternoon on all-hit radio WBBX, where you're never more than an hour away from a mega-rock-block!" Joe threw another switch to start the PSA and pulled off his headphones. From the speaker on the wall a woman's

3

voice read a message while music played in the background.

"I've got a question," Chet said, hooking his thumb toward the speaker. "How come we can't hear that speaker while you're on the air?"

"Because," Joe said, "it cuts off automatically whenever I turn on my microphone. Otherwise, we'd get feedback—and you know what that sounds like."

"You mean," Frank asked, "like when a band puts its microphones too close to the amplifiers at a rock concert?"

"Oh, yeah," Chet said. "I've heard that a few dozen times. Eeeooow!"

"You got it," Joe said. "If I did that on the air, I'd be fired in two seconds flat. Fortunately, this equipment won't let me."

"But how do you know what the record you're playing sounds like while the microphone is still on?" Frank asked. "Can you hear anything at all until you turn the microphone off?"

"Sure," Joe said. "I hear everything through my headphones, where it won't interfere with the microphone. That's why I wear them."

"So what are we listening to through that speaker?" Chet asked. "Is it hooked up straight to those CD players?"

"That speaker is attached to a monitor that picks up WBBX's signal straight off the air," Joe said, "just like a regular radio. That way we can hear what the station sounds like to our listeners."

4

"Actually," Frank said, "that speaker's turned up so loud I can barely hear anything else. Think you can make it a little softer?"

"Sure," Joe said, twiddling a knob on the console. "I'll just pot down a little."

"You'll just . . . what?" Chet asked.

"Pot down," Joe repeated. He gestured toward the knob that he'd just turned. "That's radio talk. This knob is called a potentiometer, but we call it a 'pot' for short. When you turn it down, you say that you're 'potting down.' When you turn it up—"

"You say that you're 'potting up,'" Frank finished. "I think I'm beginning to catch on to this. Maybe I can get a job here."

"Well," Joe said with a sly smile, "the job requires a little talent, too."

"Hey, I'm your brother," Frank said. "Talent runs in our family."

"Talent for what?" Chet asked innocently. "Turning knobs? I can do that, too."

"Then it *must* be easy," Joe said. "Whoops, time to play that CD." He punched a button on the console and looked up at a clock on the wall. "Let's see, that cut's five minutes and nine seconds long. I started playing it at exactly three twenty-four and fifty-one seconds, so it should end just in time for the network news at three-thirty. Perfect backtiming!"

"Maybe this job isn't so easy," Chet said, shaking his head in amazement. "You'd need a degree in math just to figure out when to play a record."

Just then the door to the studio opened, and a man

5

in his late thirties stepped through. Joe saw it was the station manager, Bill Crandall, who had given him his job at WBBX. The station manager was slender, of average height, and wore torn, faded jeans and a tie-dyed T-shirt. He had long sleek hair pulled back in a ponytail, and a pair of rimless glasses perched on his nose. Joe thought with amusement that he looked like an aging hippy, a relic of the 1960s.

Bill smiled at the boys and pulled some papers out from under his arm. "There's my main man," he said, patting Joe on the back and grinning widely. "I just got the results of a survey conducted among radio listeners in the Bayport area. And guess what?"

"Nobody's ever heard of Joe Whatsisname?" Chet suggested.

"Get a job, Chet," Joe shot back.

"Not exactly," Crandall said, looking amused. "In fact, Joe Whatsisname—excuse me, Joe Hardy—now has the highest rated show in his time slot among listeners age twelve to twenty-five."

"Hey, that's great," Frank said.

"You bet it is," Crandall said. "That's the demographic—the age group—we've been targeting. And Joe's been bringing them in by the truckload. In fact, the ratings on this time slot have increased fifteen percent since the last announcer left. Now we'll be able to raise our advertising rates. Keep on rocking, Joe. I'd say you've got a great future in radio."

Joe shrugged. "Hey, it's just natural talent. A touch of genius. A smidgen of charisma."

"And an ego as large as an astcroid," Frank added.

"That doesn't hurt," Bill Crandall agreed. "It takes a pretty strong ego to talk into a microphone knowing that there are thousands of people out there listening to your every word. Believe me, I used to do it myself."

"Thousands of people?" Joe said, raising an eyebrow. "I never thought about *thousands* of people listening to me."

"Uh-oh," Frank said. "Don't start getting stage fright, bro."

"Yeah, Joe," Chet said. "Remember the time you went on that TV talk show and got so scared you couldn't speak?"

Joe frowned. "That was a long time ago. I'm more experienced now."

"That's what you think," Frank teased.

"That's what I *know*," Joe said. "By the way," he added, turning to Crandall, "this wise guy is my brother, Frank. I told him he could hang out in the studio today, but I think from now on I'll let him listen at home."

"Glad to meet you, Frank," Crandall said. "If I have any more slots open in the future, maybe I'll give you a call. I wouldn't mind having another Hardy brother at the station."

"What about me?" Chet asked. "I think I'd make a great deejay."

"Sure," Joe said. "On the planet Spazzo."

"Are you a Hardy, too?" Crandall asked.

"Nah," Chet said. "Chet Morton, at your service."

"Chet's our best friend," Frank added. "We never go anywhere without him."

"Especially not to dinner," Joe added. "Or lunch. He frequently shows up for breakfast, too."

"Joe," Crandall said, pointing at the clock, "isn't it about time for the three-thirty news?"

"Huh?" Joe followed Crandall's gaze toward the clock. The hour and minute hands were pointing right at three-thirty, while the second hand was one notch short of the zero.

"Yowsa! You're right!" Joe exclaimed. He dived for the console. Just as the second hand touched the zero, he punched a button to turn off the CD and brought up the news broadcast from the satellite. His heart thumping, Joe sagged against the console with relief. Once again, his quick reflexes had saved him from disaster. From the speaker on the wall, the faint sounds of the newscast could be heard.

"So much for my great career in broadcasting," Joe said, catching his breath. "Now I'll be lucky if I can get my old job in advertising back."

"No problem," Crandall said. "You got the news on in time. Of course," Crandall said, chuckling, "if you'd been one second later . . ."

"Poof!" Chet said.

"I have great faith in you, Joe," Crandall said. "And we all blow it once in a while. Anyway, I'd love to hang with you guys, but I've got to get back to work. Unlike Joe, they don't pay me to spend the day talking." Bill Crandall nodded to the three teenagers, then slipped back through the studio's single door.

As soon as the station manager was gone, Joe leaned back in his chair and sighed. "Whew! I almost messed that up in a big way."

"Hey," Chet said, "You've made it this far without making a serious mistake. Give yourself a break. Being a deejay is more complicated than just spinning records."

"I wouldn't worry about it too much," Frank told his brother. "That Crandall guy seems to like you. He'll cut you some slack. Everybody makes mistakes."

"Sure," Chet said. "I bet even Bill Crandall messed up a few times when he first got on the air."

"I guess you're right," Joe said. He stood up and walked to the shelf unit again. "Guess I'd better pick out one more song for the end of my slot." He began working his way through the rows of CDs, then pulled out a Rolling Stones CD.

"Oh, don't play that," Chet said. "We've heard the Stones a million times. Why don't you play some Loup Garou?"

"Who are they?" Joe and Frank asked at the same time. Chet had a tendency to get interested in some new band every other week, and the Hardys couldn't always keep up with him.

"You don't know Loup Garou?" Chet said, looking at the Hardys as though they'd lost their minds.

Suddenly the door to the studio flew open, slamming against the back wall of the room. Joe looked up, startled to see Bill Crandall standing in the doorway. His eyes were wide, and he was panting as though he had just run all the way down the hall from his office.

"Is the monitor on?" he shouted. "Are you listening to what's going out over the air?"

"No," Joe said. "We turned the monitor down earlier."

"Uh-oh," Chet said. "You didn't hit the wrong button or something, did you, Joe?"

"It's nothing like that," Crandall said, elbowing Chet aside to get at the console. He twisted the knob that Joe had used to control the monitor.

A raspy voice echoed down from the overhead speaker. It was neither the voice of a network newscaster nor one of WBBX's announcers. Joe and Frank shot each other a quizzical look as the cackling voice continued.

"Ahoy, mateys!" the mystery deejay cried. "This is Skull and Bones Radio! We hope ye'll enjoy listening to us, all of you Bayport rock 'n' rollers. Because your former favorite radio station, the one and only WBBX, just walked the plank!"

Joe and Chet exchanged a wide-eyed glance. Both were amazed at what they were hearing.

"That's right, my friends," the voice continued. "WBBX is dead, dead, dead! And Skull and Bones just killed it!"

2 Pirates of the Airwaves

Frank Hardy stared up at the speaker in astonishment. "Where in the world is *that* coming from?" he asked.

Grimacing, Bill Crandall desperately turned the knobs on the studio console and flicked every switch back and forth, but nothing happened. The voice of Skull and Bones Radio still cackled down from the speaker overhead.

"And now, mateys," the pirate deejay gleefully announced, "for your listening enjoyment, we'll play the first of many rock 'n' roll favorites that you'll hear on Skull and Bones Radio in the months and years to come."

"Months and years?" Joe groaned. "What's this guy talking about?"

11

"They're jamming our signal," Bill Crandall said, his head hanging in frustration. "There's no way I can stop him."

"Jamming WBBX's signal?" Chet asked. "Can he do that?"

"You bet he can," Crandall said. "We broadcast at three thousand watts, so all he has to do is broadcast at a higher power and he can knock us right off the air. The engineer's in the transmitter room, but I don't think there's anything he can do."

"But it's not legal to jam a signal," Frank said.

"No," Crandall said. "It's against the law. But if this guy's clever, he'll be awfully hard to catch."

The phone near the console rang, and Joe reached for it. "The listeners are going to be calling like crazy to find out what's happening," he said as he picked up the receiver. After greeting the caller, Joe said, "I'm sure our engineer will have the problem taken care of any minute now." Then Joe got rid of the caller after taking a request.

"I'll have the switchboard operator stop these calls from coming through," Crandall said as he pressed a button for the operator's desk.

"Skull and Bones is a weird name for a radio station," Chet said after Crandall had hung up. "I thought radio stations all had names beginning with W."

"Or K, if they're west of the Mississippi River," Joe added. "I had to learn that when I took the test for my broadcasting license."

"It's a good name for a *pirate* radio station," Crandall said, "and that's apparently what this is. Pirate stations are illegal—they don't play by the rules like the rest of us do. They don't have broadcasting licenses, and sometimes they have no regard for other stations."

Hard-driving music poured out of the speaker as the four guys stared up at it. Finally Joe broke the silence. "So, what do I do now? I've been knocked off the air."

"Come on down to my office," Crandall suggested. "I've got to talk to you and Frank."

"What about me?" Chet asked.

"I need to talk to the Hardys in private, Chet. Why don't you take a walk around the station?" Crandall suggested. "We'll be back in a few minutes."

"Well, okay," Chet said. He wandered down the hall, and Joe heard him muttering something about looking for a snack bar.

Crandall told a red-haired woman named Didi, who had the next shift, to take over in the studio. Then the station manager led the Hardys to his office. Frank glanced around as Bill ushered them inside. The office was small, but it had a kind of cluttered friendliness about it. There were posters on the walls advertising rock concerts that the station had sponsored, most of them from several years before. Frank recognized signed photographs of famous rock performers. There was even an old forty-five record mounted in a frame. He looked

13

closer and realized that it was a copy of "I Am the Walrus" by the Beatles, with a label indicating that it was the first record ever played at the station.

Bill Crandall slid into a seat behind a desk that stood in front of a large window. The desk was covered with papers and broadcasting magazines, and Frank noticed that one of the stacks of papers was held down by a paperweight in the shape of a transmitting tower. The station manager gestured for the Hardys to sit in the two chairs in front of his desk. From a speaker mounted in the corner of the office, Frank could still hear the music playing dimly from the pirate radio station.

Frank watched the station manager as he settled back in his chair. There was a deeply worried look on Crandall's face.

"Have you ever dealt with a situation like this before?" Frank asked him.

"No," Crandall replied. "Though it doesn't totally surprise me. BBX is a prime target for pirates because it's such a successful station."

Crandall paused, studying Frank and Joe carefully. "I heard you kids were detectives."

"Aha," Joe said. "I see our reputation has preceded us."

"Well," Crandall said, "let's just say that the Hardy brothers are pretty well known around Bayport. I'd heard about a couple of your cases before you started working here. I hoped I wouldn't need to hire you—as detectives, anyway. But I guess the time has come."

14

"So, do you know anything at all about this pirate radio station?" Frank asked. "Do you have any idea who's behind it? Or why they're broadcasting on the same frequency as WBBX?"

"All I know," Crandall said, "is what's on this piece of paper." He pulled a sheet of paper from one of the stacks on his desk and held it out to Frank.

Frank took the paper in hand. On it were printed a few short sentences, in block letters.

"'Skull and Bones Radio is on its way,'" Frank read aloud from the sheet. "Our musical mission: to blast WBBX off the air! Stay tuned to your own frequency for more exciting developments. You'll know us when you hear us—Jolly Roger.'"

"Where'd you get that?" Joe asked.

"It came in the mail," Crandall told him. "And, no, there was no return address to tell me where it came from."

"Where was it postmarked?" Frank asked.

"Right here in Bayport," Crandall replied. "In fact, it may well have been mailed from one of the mailboxes near this station, judging from the zip code."

"Makes sense," Joe said. "Skull and Bones Radio must be local, or they couldn't interfere with your signal."

"You've got that right," Crandall agreed, "though I doubt that they're in the same zip code as we are. I'd guess they're probably someplace on the outskirts of Bayport."

"Did you show this to the authorities?" Frank asked.

"Oh, sure," Crandall replied. "Broadcasting problems like this are under the jurisdiction of the Federal Communications Commission. There's a branch office of the FCC not far from Bayport. I contacted them immediately, but they said that there was nothing they could do about it unless Skull and Bones actually started broadcasting. Until then, that piece of paper is considered nothing more than a crank letter."

"Well, hey," Joe said. "Give them a call now! It sounds as if Skull and Bones has gone into full gear this afternoon."

"I'll call them as soon as I finish talking with you," Crandall said, "but I'm not sure how much good it's going to do. We're talking about the FCC here, not the FBI. They simply don't have the resources to send out dozens of agents to track a pirate station to ground. They're busy dealing with the bigger stations. I'm sure they'll bust Skull and Bones Radio eventually, but by that time WBBX may be history as well."

"Uh-oh," Joe said. "There goes my job."

"I don't suppose you guys can stop broadcasting for a few months and live off your savings?" Frank suggested.

"No way," Crandall said. "We're a small radio station. Joe's been bringing in some good ratings for us, but it'll take a while before those ratings pay off. In the meantime, we're operating on a very close margin. If we have to shut down for as little as a week, we'll have to declare bankruptcy."

"Well," Joe said, "I guess if I'm going to keep my job, my brother and I are going to have to help you find this pirate radio station."

Crandall smiled for the first time since the conversation had begun. "That's what I hoped you'd say, my friend. Frank, will you go along with your brother?"

"Of course," Frank said, a slight hint of indignation in his tone. "You don't think I'd let a mystery like this slip by without trying to solve it, do you?"

"I knew you guys would give us a hand!" Crandall exclaimed. "I wish I had more clues to give you, but that sheet of paper is all I have."

"Maybe we can get some clues by listening to Skull and Bones Radio," Frank suggested as the sounds of the pirate radio station wafted down from the speaker on the wall. "Do you think you could turn that thing up?"

"Sure," Crandall said. He walked over to the speaker and turned a knob mounted underneath it. The sound of Skull and Bones Radio grew louder, but the song that was being played was just coming to an end. As it did, the cackling announcer came back on the air.

"This was just a sample of what Skull and Bones Radio has in store for ye, mateys," crowed the announcer. "But that's all the time we have today. We'll be back tomorrow—and, before ya know it, we'll be on the air twenty-four hours a day. For now, it's back to your good friends at WBBX. See you on the airwaves!"

The signal from the pirate station abruptly vanished, to be replaced by dead air. The network newscast was now long over, and the WBBX studios were engulfed in an unnatural silence for a moment. Then the deejay who had taken over for Joe came on the air.

Joe bolted to his feet. "Uh-oh! Looks like I'd better get back to the studio." He raced out of Bill Crandall's office and down the hall.

Moments after Joe exited, a middle-aged man in a striped sweater poked his head in the door. He had wavy graying hair and a slightly sour expression. "Maybe that young Joe Hardy is getting a little *too* serious about the radio business," the man said. "He almost knocked me down on his way to the studio."

"We're having a bit of an emergency," Crandall said. "I'll tell you about it later, Jack. Joe was just helping out."

"Does it have to do with that letter you got the other day?" the man asked.

"Yeah," Crandall said. "I'll stop by your office in a few minutes and fill you in."

"Was that anybody I should know?" Frank asked as soon as the visitor left.

"Oh, sorry," Crandall said. "I should have introduced you. That was Jack Ruiz, co-owner of the station. I'll introduce you to him when I get a chance."

"Okay," Frank said. "Oh, by the way, if Joe and I

18

are going to help you with this Skull and Bones case, who's going to do Joe's radio show while he's investigating?"

Crandall looked surprised by the question. "You know, I hadn't thought of that. When Skull and Bones blocked out our signal a few minutes ago, I thought we'd be off the air permanently. But now it looks as if they'll be giving us a brief reprieve before they lower the boom."

"I've got a suggestion," Frank said.

"I'm all ears," Crandall told him.

"Why not use Chet?" Frank said. "He said he was interested in becoming a deejay."

Crandall gave Frank a dubious look. "Do you think he has any talent for the job?"

"Well," Frank said, "let's just say that Chet has enthusiasm."

"Enthusiasm?" Crandall repeated. "Well, all right, if you say so. I'll ask Chet to fill in for Joe. Then we'll—"

Crandall was cut off by a sudden shattering noise. The window behind the station manager's desk was smashed as a small object hurtled through it. The object dropped to the middle of the floor and rolled right up to Frank's feet.

Frank looked down at it, gaping.

It was a hand grenade!

3 A Shocking Development

Crandall wasn't sure what had happened, because the grenade flew in from behind him and landed on the other side of his desk.

But it took Frank Hardy all of one second to take in the situation. Somebody had tossed a hand grenade through Crandall's window, it was now sitting at Frank's feet, and the pin was missing—which meant that it would explode within the next few seconds!

"Get out of here!" Frank shouted at Crandall. "Run for the hallway!" In one fluid movement Frank leapt over the hand grenade and grabbed Crandall by the arm, pulling him through the office door. He then shoved Crandall to the floor and got down alongside him.

"Ouch!" Crandall shouted. "What are you trying to do, break my ribs?"

"Get down!" Frank repeated. "That was a hand grenade. It's about to explode!"

"A . . . a hand grenade?" Crandall gasped, flattening himself against the floor. "Who'd want to throw a hand grenade into my office?"

"I don't know," Frank replied, huddling next to the station manager. "But somehow I have a feeling that not everybody loves this radio station as much as Joe and I do."

Frank put his hands over his head and rolled his body into a tight ball. Crandall did the same. The two of them waited as the clock on the wall ticked off the seconds. Frank's heart pounded loudly in his chest as he waited for the sound of the explosion. Would the wall that stood between them and the grenade be enough to protect them from the shock?

Frank never found out, because nothing happened. After about a minute had passed, Frank peered cautiously through the door into Crandall's office, craning his head to get a look at the hand grenade.

"What do you see?" Crandall asked, adjusting his glasses. "Is it going to explode?"

"It already has," Frank replied.

"What?" Crandall asked in amazement. "I didn't hear anything."

"That's because it didn't make any noise," Frank told him, rising to his feet. He stepped back into the office and walked to where the hand grenade lay in pieces on the floor among the shattered glass.

"Was it a dud?" Crandall asked, following Frank into the room. "Maybe there wasn't enough explosive in it."

"I don't think there was *any* explosive in it," Frank said, crouching on the floor. "It doesn't look like it was meant to cause damage. It's a fake, a dummy grenade."

He began examining the grenade. It appeared to have burst apart into four neatly divided pieces. Apparently there was a spring inside that had popped it open a few seconds after it hit the floor, while Crandall and Frank were huddled outside the office. In the middle of the pieces was a folded sheet of paper. Frank picked it up and began to read.

"'Skull and Bones Radio is out to destroy WBBX,'" he began. "'How do you like us so far? Enjoy your last moments on the air. Within a few days Skull and Bones will start broadcasting full-time, and WBBX will be drowned out forever. Got that, mateys?—Jolly Roger.'"

Crandall sighed deeply. "This Jolly Roger jerk, whoever he is, is definitely out to get us."

"And we might have a chance to catch him!" Frank exclaimed, suddenly leaping to his feet. "If he just threw this in the window, maybe he's still outside."

"Good," Crandall said. "See if you can catch him while I call the police."

Frank raced out of the office and through the front door of the small building that contained the WBBX studios. Outside, a short sidewalk led from the front door to the street. On one side the WBBX building was attached directly to the row of buildings next door—a video rental store, a print shop, and several fast-food businesses. On the other, the side where Crandall's office was located, a small alley ran next to the building. Frank ran halfway down the sidewalk, looked down the street, then changed course and headed toward the alley. Before he reached it, he saw somebody come walking out of it.

The man in the alley looked to be in his late twenties. He wore dirty blue jeans and a T-shirt with the name of a heavy metal rock band silk-screened on it. Dark stubble covered his cheeks and chin, as though he hadn't shaved for a couple of days. Now that's suspicious timing, Frank thought, sizing the guy up. The man glared at Frank, then continued walking toward the street.

"Hey!" Frank shouted. "What are you doing there?"

"What do you mean, what am I doing here?" asked the stranger in a defensive tone. "Everybody's gotta be somewhere, man."

"Somebody just threw a hand grenade through one of the windows in that building," Frank told him. "Did you see who did it?"

"A hand grenade?" asked the stranger, an amused look crossing his face. "Has somebody been using your cranium for a conga drum, man? What does this look like, a war zone?"

Frank looked down the alley, but there was nobody else in sight. "What it looks like," Frank retorted, "is that you're the only one here. The grenade was just thrown two minutes ago. Where were you then?"

The stranger's expression grew angry. "If you're trying to lay some blame on me, man, why don't you come right out and say it? You think I threw a hand grenade, right?"

"You seem to be in the wrong place at the wrong time," Frank said, "and that makes you the prime suspect. What were you doing outside this building?"

"I used to work here," the stranger said. "Not that it's any of your business. I just stopped by to pick up my last paycheck. My name's Keith Wyatt. I'm a deejay."

"Wyatt?" Frank repeated. The name sounded familiar for some reason. "Oh, yeah—you're the guy Joe replaced."

"You mean Joe Hardy?" Wyatt said. "That wimp? He wouldn't know how to be a good deejay if he went to broadcasting school for the rest of his life."

"Hey, watch it!" Frank snapped angrily. "That's my brother you're talking about."

"Uh-oh," Wyatt sneered. "Don't tell me you're trying to get a job here, too. That's just what this station needs, two Hardys."

"I'm trying to find out who threw a grenade through the window," Frank said, "and you look like—"

Suddenly Bill Crandall emerged from the door of

24

the building. He shouted to Frank, "I called the police. They'll be here in a minute." Then he noticed the other man standing in the alley. "What's going on here, Frank? Who's this?"

Wyatt turned toward the station manager and, with a smirk, said, "Hello, Bill. Remember me? I wish I could say it was good to see you again."

"What are you doing around here, Wyatt?" Crandall asked, walking toward them. "I thought I asked you not to come back to this station."

"I've got a right to pick up my paycheck, don't I?" Wyatt said. "Believe me, you won't be seeing me around here anymore."

"You know this guy?" Frank asked. "I found him out here in the alley, right after that grenade came through the window."

"You still think I had something to do with that?" Wyatt asked. "Okay, I *did* hear something that sounded like breaking glass just before I left the building. But by the time I walked over to the alley to take a look, there was nobody around. Satisfied?"

"I'm not sure I am," Frank said.

Wyatt started to make an angry retort, but at that moment a police car pulled into the alley from behind the building, and he held his tongue. Two young officers, one male and one female, stepped out of the squad car and walked over to the trio.

"Are you the ones who called in a vandalism report?" the woman asked.

"I am," Crandall said. "Someone threw a dummy hand grenade through an office window."

25

"Do you have the grenade?" the man asked.

"Yes," Crandall said. "Follow me and I'll show you."

Crandall led the male officer inside while the other officer stayed in the alley to question Frank and Keith Wyatt. Although Frank voiced his suspicions about the former radio announcer, the officer determined that there wasn't enough evidence against Wyatt to warrant an arrest. Moments later the second officer returned from inside the WBBX building with Bill Crandall. After taking down everybody's names, the two officers climbed into the squad car together and drove away.

"Well," Wyatt said, "I think it's time for me to get out of here. Unless you two guys like me so much that you can't stand to see me go."

"I've still got some questions I want to ask you," Frank said.

"Well, ask them some other time," Wyatt replied. "I've got places to go and people to see." Wyatt turned away from Frank and Crandall and strolled casually across the street.

There is something about this Wyatt guy that I really don't like, Frank thought. But it was true that there was no direct evidence that he had thrown the grenade, at least none that had been uncovered yet. Maybe if the police turned up Wyatt's fingerprints on the grenade . . . But somehow Frank had a feeling that wasn't going to happen.

Frank turned back to Crandall. "That guy told me

he used to work here," he said. "Is that true? Is he the guy Joe replaced?"

"That's right," Crandall said. "The one and only Keith Wyatt."

Frank glanced down at the pavement where Wyatt had been standing. There was a scrap of colored cardboard lying on the ground. He bent down and picked it up, turning it over in his fingers. It was a small matchbook, the kind that might be found on the counter in a restaurant or diner.

"What's that?" Crandall asked.

"I think our friend Wyatt left a souvenir behind," Frank said, holding out the matchbook for Crandall to see. "It's got something written on it, too. 'The Seven-Thirty Club.'"

"Oh, yeah," Crandall said. "That's a small joint a few blocks from here, where Wyatt hangs around with some of the bums that he calls his friends." Crandall shook his head in disgust.

"I gather there's no love lost between you and him," Frank said as they walked back into the building together.

"No, there isn't," Crandall agreed. "Wyatt's a bum just like his friends. Always arrived late for his show, left early. He has no sense of responsibility. I yelled at him a thousand times, and then one day he didn't show up at all. I put Joe on the air in his place. When Wyatt appeared the next day, I fired him on the spot and gave the job to Joe—at least until I can find a permanent replacement."

"Did he say why he hadn't been in the day before?" Frank asked.

"He claimed his grandmother had died," Crandall scoffed.

"Well," Frank said doubtfully, "I guess that's possible."

"He'd used that lame excuse at least a dozen times before. I just wasn't willing to put up with him anymore."

"I can't blame you," Frank said, feeling sorry for anyone who had to put up with Keith Wyatt. "Do you think he holds a grudge against you? Could he have something to do with this Skull and Bones station, maybe as a way of getting revenge?"

"I'd say he's too lazy to start something like that himself, but he could be involved in it," Crandall said. "I wouldn't put it past him."

They had arrived at the door to Crandall's office. Crandall reached out to grip the door handle, then glanced at his watch instead.

"It's almost the end of Joe's shift," the station manager told Frank. "Why don't we go down to the studio and help him get things wrapped up?"

"Good idea," Frank said. "The sooner we get out of here, the sooner we can start trying to crack this Skull and Bones mystery."

They entered the studio just as Joe was punching up the four o'clock network newscast. Didi, the deejay whose show followed Joe's, was shuffling through the stacks of CDs. Chet was munching on a hamburger and fries that he had ordered at a take-out place nearby.

"Be with you in a second, guys," Joe said as he filled in the FCC logs with what he'd played that day. "Let me get everything straightened up, then I'm outta here." He looked up in annoyance at the speaker on the wall as the newscast blared out of it. "Someone must have turned that thing up while I was out of the room," he said. "It's been driving me crazy, but I didn't have time to fix it while I was on the air. Let me turn it down before somebody goes deaf."

Joe reached out to the knob that controlled the speaker. Suddenly there was a loud crackling sound, followed by a shriek of pain from Joe. A bright spark of electricity jumped off the knob, and Joe was propelled backward across the room.

With a thud he fell to the floor in the middle of the studio, unconscious!

4 The 7:30 Club

The last thing Joe could remember was reaching up to turn the knob on the console. Then, as if by magic, he found himself on the floor of the room, with four panicked faces looking down at him.

His brother, Frank, was reaching out to slap him.

"Hey!" Joe shouted, shooting out a hand to catch Frank by the wrist. "What do you think you're doing?"

"Trying to wake you up," Frank said, a note of alarm in his voice. "You were out like a light."

"I was?" Joe said fuzzily. He shook his head, but it didn't help to clear it. Had he really been unconscious? Well, that would certainly explain what he was doing on the floor. And why his head felt as though somebody had been sticking needles in it.

"Maybe you're right," Joe said. "What happened?"

"It looked like you took a bad shock," Crandall said. "There must have been a loose wire on the console, and your hand brushed against it when you went to turn the knob."

"Hmm, I wonder about that," Frank said. He stood and walked over to the console. "No, I don't think that's quite what happened," he said. "Somebody set this up deliberately."

Joe pulled himself up to a sitting position. "Deliberately? How can you tell?"

"Look at this," Frank said, pointing to a wire on the console. "This wire is wrapped around the base of the knob. You could hardly have touched the knob without touching the wire—and getting yourself electrocuted."

"But that wasn't there when I turned the speaker down earlier," Joe said.

"Right," Frank said. "Somebody must have done some fancy wiring when you were out of the room."

Joe climbed back to his feet. He felt a little unsteady, but the wooziness was already starting to vanish.

"Are you okay, Joe?" Crandall asked. "Should I call a doctor? Or an ambulance?"

"Nah, that's all right," Joe said shakily. "I'll be okay."

"I'd suggest you get somebody to remove this wire from the knob," Frank said, "before more of your announcers get fried."

31

"*I'd* certainly appreciate that," Didi said as she sat in the swivel chair and put on the headset.

"I'll take care of it right away," Crandall said.

"I hope you guys don't mind," said Didi, plugging a CD into one of the players, "but I've got to do my show now."

"Right," Joe said. "We were just leaving."

Outside the doorway Crandall said goodbye to the brothers, then went off to find the engineer. Chet leaned against the wall and stuffed the last of his burger into his mouth.

"So who do you suppose wired that knob?" Frank asked Joe. "You were in the studio most of the time, weren't you?"

"Well," Joe said, "I was out of the studio for about five or ten minutes checking the Teletype and fax machines. That would have been enough time to rig the wire. Didi wasn't in the studio until a few minutes ago. And Crandall was with you all the time."

"Hey, Chet," Frank said. "When you were wandering around the station, did you notice anything suspicious?"

"Yeah," said their husky friend with a nod. "The soda machine here is completely out of cola. I had to go outside to get something to drink."

"What Frank means," Joe said, "is did you see anybody suspicious hanging around the studio while I was gone?"

"As a matter of fact, I did," Chet said. "Well, I don't know if you'd call him suspicious or not, but I saw this guy in a striped sweater go in there for a moment, then come back out."

"Striped sweater?" Joe asked. "You mean Jack Ruiz?"

"Oh, yeah," Frank said. "The co-owner of the station. I met him in Crandall's office, sort of. I wonder what he was doing in there?"

"Could have been anything," Joe said. "He's in and out all the time. He checks the on-air log to see what commercials were played, and he changes the messages on the bulletin board."

"And maybe he wired the knob to electrocute one of his disc jockeys?" Frank suggested.

"Doesn't sound likely to me," Joe said. "He's part owner of the station, after all. Did you see anybody else go in the studio, Chet?"

"Nope," Chet said, "but I wasn't there the whole time. Anybody could have slipped in and out while I was gone."

"True," Frank said. "Ever hear of a guy named Keith Wyatt?"

"Sure," Joe said. "He's the guy I replaced."

"Right," Frank said. "How did you and Wyatt get along?"

"We didn't see each other a lot," Joe said, "but he didn't like the fact that Crandall and I got along so well."

"Well, I just saw Wyatt outside the station," Frank said. "In fact, I think he may have pitched a phony hand grenade through Bill Crandall's window."

"What?" Joe exclaimed. "Hand grenade? When did this happen?"

Frank quickly described the incident in Crandall's office, continuing the story up to the point where the police refused to arrest Wyatt without further evidence.

"It sure sounds as if he had the opportunity and the motive to pitch the grenade," Joe said. "And if he was in the building to pick up his check, he could have slipped into the studio and wired the knob."

"I think we should talk to this Wyatt guy," Frank said. "Don't you?"

"You bet," Joe said. "The problem is finding him."

Frank reached into his pocket and pulled out the matchbook that he had found in the alley. "I think it might be easier than we think," Frank said. "He goes to a place called the Seven-Thirty Club."

"Oh, yeah," Joe said sourly. "It's a real dive, in a crummy neighborhood. Not the kind of place where you'd want to hang out, unless you had a large, vicious dog with you."

"I don't know where we'll turn up a dog on such short notice," Frank said. "So I guess we'll have to get by on our wits."

"Then you're in a lot of trouble," Chet joked.

"Thanks a lot," Frank said. "And I was just about to ask if you wanted to come along, too."

"That's okay," Chet said. "I promised Callie and Iola that we'd meet them over at Mr. Pizza after Joe's shift." Callie Shaw was Frank's steady girlfriend, and Joe dated Iola Morton, Chet's sister.

34

"Whoops," Joe said. "That's right. We did promise them."

"Well," Frank said, "tell them we'll be late."

"Yeah," Joe added. "Tell the girls we've already got a dinner date in a real classy joint."

Joe stared out of the passenger-side window at the 7:30 Club as Frank drove their converted police van down the street, looking for a parking spot. To call this neighborhood run-down, thought Joe, would be a compliment. It was a dump. A neon sign with the name of the restaurant and a picture of a clock blinked and sputtered in the front window. Half of the letters in the name of the club were no longer illuminated, so that it read "7 3 Cl b."

"I hope this place looks better on the inside than it does on the outside," Joe said.

"It could hardly look worse," Frank replied.

"I wouldn't bet on that," Joe said sourly.

Frank pulled the van into a parking place about half a block from the club. The Hardys climbed out, carefully locking the van door behind them, and walked toward the front door of the 7:30 Club. Joe opened the door to the restaurant and stepped inside, his brother directly behind him.

The interior was dark, but Joe could see a long bar, where a couple of individuals sipped drinks. There were tables scattered about, but the chairs surrounding them were empty. A sour odor hung in the air, and something sticky on the floor caused their feet to make popping noises as they walked.

Against one wall a trio of musicians played loud rock music. In the back of the club, where three pool tables had been set up, a group of men were playing pool or lounging around talking.

"There he is," Frank said, spotting Keith Wyatt in a corner of the room. "Let's go talk to him."

"I hate to point this out," Joe said, "but if these are his friends, they've got us outnumbered."

"We're not here to get into a fight with him," Frank pointed out. "We're here to ask him questions."

"Yeah," Joe said. "That's how it always starts out."

Wyatt saw the Hardys coming as they walked toward him across the room. "Well, if it isn't the Hardy twins," he said with a laugh. "Hardydum and Hardydee."

Joe felt a flash of anger at Wyatt's words, but his brother placed an arm on his shoulder and whispered, "Let's just ask questions, remember?"

"So what do you two want?" Wyatt asked. "Did you stop by to play a few rounds of pool?"

"We just want to talk with you, Keith," Frank said. "There's a couple of things we need to know."

"Like what?" Wyatt asked. "Like whether I threw that grenade through Crandall's window?"

"I don't remember telling you that it was Bill Crandall's window," Frank said.

"Oh, you're real sharp," Wyatt said, laughing again. "It wasn't hard to figure whose window got trashed. I saw the broken glass outside Crandall's office, and he was the one who called the cops. What

36

I want to know is, why are you guys so interested in finding out who threw that grenade? What business is it of yours?"

"That's not the only thing we're interested in," Joe said. "We also want to find out about a pirate radio station called Skull and Bones. You know anything about it?"

Wyatt stopped smiling and stared at the Hardys. "Maybe I do and maybe I don't. Why should I tell you?"

"Because Joe and I have decided to get a job there," Frank said. Joe gave Frank a funny look but said nothing. "We thought you could help us."

Wyatt sneered at Frank. "You expect me to believe that? Joe's got a cushy job at BBX. Why would he give that up?"

"I'm getting bored at BBX," Joe said, going along with Frank's story. "This pirate radio station sounds really cool."

Wyatt laughed again. Joe couldn't stand seeing him bare his yellow teeth every time he pulled his lips back to smile. Then the former announcer shrugged and said, "Hey, I might as well tell you about Skull and Bones. I'm not working there, so what do I care?"

He led the Hardys to a table and sat down. "I got this call from some guy named Jimmy Collins, who said he was looking for deejays for a new station. He'd heard I was out of work, asked me if I wanted a job. I told him I was interested. But then I found out through the grapevine that he was running a pirate station, on board some ship anchored outside Barmet Bay. He wanted me to meet him down at a place called the Bayside Warehouse. But I told him no thanks."

"How come?" Joe asked.

"I don't want to work for somebody who might disappear before he writes me my first paycheck," Wyatt said. "I'm looking for legitimate radio work— if I can still find any after all the lies that jerk Bill Crandall has spread about me."

"Lies?" Frank asked.

"Yeah," Wyatt said. "He's spread rumors around the industry that I'm lazy and unreliable. I ought to sue the pants off Crandall!" Wyatt turned his gaze on Joe. "Hey, maybe you could vouch for me with some other radio stations, tell them what a good announcer I am."

"I wouldn't want to lie," Joe replied, immediately regretting his choice of words.

"Why you—!" Wyatt rose angrily from the table. "I told your brother that you were the wimpiest deejay in town, and I was right. You probably helped spread the lies that got me fired, so you could get my job."

"That's not true," Joe said. "Crandall could see what an untrustworthy deejay you were just by opening his eyes."

"I ought to tear you apart for that remark!" Wyatt snapped.

"Tear me apart?" Joe responded. "I'd like to see you try."

38

Frank grabbed Joe by the shoulder and pulled him away from the table. "Hey, we didn't come here to fight, just to ask questions."

"I didn't start this fight," Joe said.

"Yeah," Wyatt said, "because you're a coward."

"What did you call me?" Joe snapped back.

"He's too smart to get into a fight," Frank said, pulling his reluctant brother across the room. "Aren't you, Joe?"

"Speak for yourself," Joe yelled to Wyatt, though he allowed Frank to yank him steadily toward the entrance.

They were almost to the front door when a pool ball whizzed through the air past Joe's shoulder. It smashed through the thin wood of the door with an explosive sound, sending splinters flying through the air.

Then a second pool ball came whistling after it, this one aimed straight at Joe's head!

5 The S.S. Marconi

"Heads up!" Frank shouted desperately.

"You mean *heads down!*" Joe cried as he ducked beneath the pool ball. This time the ball smashed into the front window, sending shards of glass flying in all directions.

"Hey!" someone yelled. Frank saw a stout middle-aged man in a cook's apron appear from behind the counter. "Cut that out! You're tearing the place up!"

"Shut up, old man," cracked somebody in the back of the room. Frank looked up to see three large figures moving toward him from the pool tables. The one in the lead was about thirty years old, with a large belly sticking out from his T-shirt and a fuzzy red beard that hung down over his chest like a bib. He would have been a comical figure, Frank thought,

40

except that he had an impressive set of muscles above the belly. And the thick wooden pool cue that he was slapping against the palm of his left hand could turn out to be a dangerous weapon.

"Sounds to me like you two have been giving our friend Keith a hard time," Redbeard said. "Ain't that right, guys?"

"Sounds right to me," said one of the two muscular guys standing behind him.

"I'm with you, Red," the other chimed in.

"It was a minor difference of opinion," Frank said. "We were just leaving, anyway."

"Oh, is that right?" Redbeard said, walking toward Frank and Joe with the pool cue held upright. "Well, maybe it's not quite time for you to leave yet."

"Hey, fuzz face!" Joe replied sharply. "Who are you to tell us what to do? My brother and I can leave anytime we want to."

"What did you call me?" Redbeard said, his face flushing to almost the same color as his hair. "I think it's time I taught you a lesson, wimp."

Redbeard swung the pool cue at Joe, who sprang back just far enough to avoid getting whacked. The sharp breeze from its passage whistled across his face from cheek to cheek, a hint of what the cue would have done to him if it had connected.

Frank pulled open the front door and said quietly to Joe, "Let's get out of here. Not only do these guys have us outnumbered, they're better armed than we are."

"Let's get 'em, guys!" Redbeard yelled, as the

41

Hardys dashed through the front door and out onto the sidewalk. Frank noticed that, despite the red-bearded leader's considerable bulk, he was fast on his feet.

"Head for the van," Frank said, pulling his keychain from his pocket. "You hold them off while I unlock the door."

"Oh, thanks a lot," Joe said, running directly behind his brother. "Why am I the one who gets to hold them off?"

"Because I've got the keys, dummy," Frank said over his shoulder as he ran up to the passenger-side door of the van. Joe spun around to see that the trio from the bar was still directly behind him.

"I've got you now!" Redbeard shouted as Joe turned to face him. Redbeard started to swing the cue stick at Joe, but he feinted with a sharp karate kick that caused his plump attacker to hesitate in mid-swing. The kick never connected, but Redbeard's brief pause allowed Joe to yank the pool cue out of his hand.

"Who's got who now?" Joe shouted, swinging the pool cue back at his attacker. "Now the pool cue's in the other hand, fuzz face!"

Redbeard jumped backward, nearly stumbling into his two companions as they rushed up behind him. Meanwhile, Frank twisted the key into the lock and yanked the van door open.

"Get in, fast!" he yelled as he clambered over the gearshift and tumbled into the driver's seat.

42

"I'm on my way," Joe replied, taking one last swipe at Redbeard with the pool cue. Then he turned around, leapt into the passenger seat, and started to close the door even as Frank was gunning the van into the street.

But Joe never got the door closed. Redbeard grabbed the door handle and mounted one foot on the doorstep, seemingly unconcerned that the van was moving. He balled his free hand into a fist and sent it flying toward Joe's chin.

Joe pulled his head back just as Redbeard's knuckles swished past. "How'd you get in here?" Joe shouted.

"I ain't letting you get away so easy!" Redbeard shouted in return. He grabbed the back of Joe's seat and tried to pull himself bodily into the van.

"Oh, no, you don't," Frank said, swerving the van back and forth across the empty street. Redbeard started to fall backward through the door but managed to keep a grip on the van.

"You can't shake me off that easy," Redbeard said, preparing to pull himself into the van a second time.

"Wanna bet?" Joe said, swiveling around in his seat so that the soles of his shoes were pointed directly at the man. He pulled his knees up tightly under his chin, then kicked out with all his strength at Redbeard's chest.

With a gasp the pool player lost his grip and fell away from the van. He flew through the air for a fraction of a second, then landed with a thud on a stack of trash cans that someone had left next to the curb. The last that the Hardys saw of him, he was trying to fight his way out of a pile of garbage.

"Let's hope we don't run into him again," Joe said.

"Next time," Frank said, "let's meet Keith Wyatt on less dangerous turf."

The Hardys spent the rest of the evening at Mr. Pizza with their girlfriends, Callie and Iola, and of course Chet. They told the story of their encounter at the 7:30 Club several times, to the laughs and gasps of their audience. Finally, at nine o'clock they announced that they had a big day of detective work ahead of them and that they had to get home.

The next morning, gathered around a heaping breakfast of their aunt Gertrude's pancakes, the brothers began making plans for catching Jolly Roger and locating Skull and Bones Radio.

"So what do you think of the stuff that Keith Wyatt told us?" Frank asked as he poured syrup on his plate. "Do you think Jimmy Collins really exists? Could that be the real name of this character who calls himself Jolly Roger?"

"Maybe," Joe said. "And what about this Bayside Warehouse?"

"That shouldn't be too hard to track down," Frank said. "We'll look it up in the phone book. If only you and Wyatt hadn't gotten into a shouting match last night, we might have found out even more."

"Oh, great," Joe said. "Don't put the blame on me. Wyatt was acting like a turkey!"

Frank walked to the telephone stand and picked up a phone book, then brought it back to the table.

"Let's see," he said, thumbing through the pages. "Here we go—Bayside Warehouse. It's located on Bayside Drive."

"Where else?" Joe said. "I think it's time we took a little trip down to the bay." He stuffed the last piece of pancake into his mouth.

"Right," Frank said. "After all, where else would pirates hang out?"

Within a half hour the Hardys had parked the dark blue van along Bayside Drive, one half of which was lined with buildings, the other with a wooden pier that ran along the bayfront.

Joe Hardy took a deep breath of salty air and gazed out over the sparkling waters. It was a beautiful summer morning, with clear blue skies overhead and a cool breeze in the air. "Nice day for a cruise, don't you think?" he said, turning to his brother.

"As long as we know where we're cruising to," Frank said.

"Maybe the folks at Bayside Warehouse will have some idea," Joe said. "Let's pay them a visit."

The brothers strolled along the sidewalk opposite the pier, toward a long low building with a sign identifying it as Bayside Warehouse.

"This looks like the place," Frank said.

"Wonder if anybody's home," Joe said.

45

The warehouse had two doors, a wide delivery door and a small door set next to it. At the moment both were closed. Joe walked up to the small door and knocked on it loudly.

"What are you looking for?" asked a sharp voice. To Joe's surprise, the voice wasn't coming from inside the warehouse. It was coming from the pier, behind him. He turned to see an old man standing on the aft end of a small tugboat lashed to the pier with a rope. The old man had weatherbeaten skin, a sour look on his face, and he wore a badly stained workshirt and overalls.

Joe started walking across Bayside Drive toward the old man. "We, uh, heard that we might be able to find a job in radio here," he said, feeling foolish as he said it. Finding a radio job on the docks? That was such a silly idea that he expected to hear the old man break out in raucous laughter.

Instead, the old man stared at him with a hostile expression. "And who told you such a thing?" he asked.

"Jimmy Collins," Frank blurted. "Uh, Jimmy Collins told us that we should come down here to Bayside Warehouse."

"Collins, eh?" the old man growled. "Why didn't he tell me about this?"

"I, uh, don't know," Joe said. "Maybe he forgot."

"He probably didn't have time," Frank added. "He asked us to come down here in a hurry. And he probably didn't have a chance to let you know."

The old man spat angrily over the side of the

tugboat, into the bay. "Why should Collins care?" he snapped. "I'm nothin' but the hired help to him. Why should he tell me about anything ahead of time? I'll have a little talk with him when we get back."

"Get back?" Joe asked.

"To the ship," the old man said. "You are coming along with me, aren't you?"

Frank and Joe exchanged glances. "Uh, yeah, I guess we are."

"Then get on board," the old man told them. "Or are you going to stand there like a pair of buoys, bobbing in the wind?"

Joe took a tentative step onto the tugboat, followed a moment later by Frank. "Well," Joe whispered to his brother, "I did say that it would be a great day for a cruise."

"Yeah," Frank whispered in reply. "I'm glad we could find a luxury yacht like this to take it on."

"Excuse me, sir. Mind if I ask your name?" Joe said as the old man began unknotting the rope that lashed the tugboat to the pier.

"Steelhart," the old man said. "Captain Steelhart. Didn't Collins tell you anything?"

Joe looked around at the inside of the tug. The deck was made of corrugated metal and was covered with a thick veneer of dried grease and mud. Frayed old ropes were scattered across it, and half a dozen unmarked metal barrels were lined against one side.

Captain Steelhart finished untying the ship from the pier, then walked to the forward end of the tug, where a door led into a small cabin. He stepped inside, and a moment later a motor began to chug noisily. The tug lurched out into the bay.

They headed for the middle of the bay for about ten minutes, then turned toward the Atlantic Ocean. Before long, the mouth of the bay appeared, and the tugboat plowed into the open sea.

After they'd gone about ten miles or so out into the Atlantic, Frank pointed off into the distance. "Look," he said. "I wonder if that's what we're headed for."

Joe looked where Frank was indicating. In the distance he could see the rusted old hulk of a merchant ship. The sides were painted a faded blue and gray. The deck of the ship rode about thirty feet above the water, and several structures were visible along its hundred-foot length. It scarcely looked seaworthy, yet it showed no sign of sinking as the ocean waves splashed against its sides. As they drew closer, they could even make out a name freshly painted on its bow: The S.S. *Marconi*.

"Marconi?" Joe asked. "Isn't he the guy who invented radio?"

"I don't think that's the original name of the ship," Frank replied. "It looks as though somebody's painted over the original name. But can you think of a better name for a ship with a pirate radio station on it?"

"How about the S.S. *Skull and Bones?*" Joe suggested.

"That might attract just a little unwanted attention from the Coast Guard," Frank said.

"Yeah," Joe said. "At least the S.S. *Marconi* is subtle."

"It couldn't be too subtle," Frank added. "You figured it out, didn't you?"

Joe gave Frank a dirty look but didn't reply. The tugboat was plowing straight toward the S.S. *Marconi*. At the last second Steelhart turned aside and brought the tug up next to the ship's rusting hull.

From above, someone lowered a sturdy-looking cable with a hook on the end of it. Steelhart emerged from his cabin and pushed the hook toward Joe.

"Here," he said. "Make yourselves useful. Help them unload the fuel barrels."

"Fuel barrels?" Joe asked.

"These, ya fool," the old man snarled, pointing at the barrels lined up against the side of the tug. "Stick the hook on them, so they can be hauled up."

Joe and Frank exchanged puzzled looks but did as they were ordered. Within a few minutes all of the barrels had been lifted onto the ship above.

"Now, go on up," Steelhart said. "You said that Jimmy Collins was waiting for you, didn't ya?"

"Oh, right," Frank said. "Are we supposed to grab one of those hooks and let them haul us up, too?"

"Climb up the hull," the old man said impatiently.

Joe looked at the hull of the ship and saw that there were rungs placed at intervals up the side, forming a kind of ladder. Taking a deep breath, he

49

grabbed the lower rung and pulled himself up. Frank followed just below him, and Steelhart followed below Frank.

When Joe reached the top, he climbed over a railing and onto the deck of the ship. The S.S. *Marconi* was in better shape than the small tug that had brought them there, but not much. The deck was grimy, and paint was peeling off the bulkheads. The barrels that had just been raised off the tug lined the deck, where a pair of burly crewmen were starting to wheel them on dollies to another part of the ship.

As Steelhart climbed over the railing, he shouted, "Collins! Get your ugly face up here. Two guys are here to see you."

After a moment a cabin door opened and a slender man of about thirty stepped out of the hatchway. He was wearing a striped silk shirt and designer jeans. His black hair was long but styled. His smile faded when he saw Frank and Joe.

"Who are these guys?" he asked Steelhart. "I wasn't expecting them."

"What?" Steelhart cried. "They told me you asked them to be here."

"Um, we're deejays, sir," Joe said. He didn't want to reveal their names in case Collins had heard his name on WBBX. "We hoped maybe we could get jobs here."

"Well, I didn't ask you to come here," Collins said. "That's for sure."

Steelhart's face turned purple with rage. "Then you lied to me!" he declared, raising a fist at the

Hardys. He turned and beckoned to the two burly crewmen. "Come here!" he told them. "Throw these two jokers overboard. That should teach them a lesson!"

The Hardys saw two crewmen begin walking toward them, menacing smiles crossing the shipmen's faces.

Gloating, the old man grinned. "It'll be the last lesson they'll ever learn!"

6 Job Interview

Frank and Joe backed toward the railing as the two burly crewmen advanced on them. Nervously Frank glanced to both sides to see if there was a nearby hiding place that he and Joe could reach before the crewmen were on top of them. Unfortunately, there was not. The Hardys would just have to hope that their quick wits would be a match for the muscles on the two deckhands.

"Wait a minute!" Jimmy Collins shouted, stepping in between the crewmen and the Hardys. "You're not going to throw these two guys overboard. I'll talk to them, decide if I have any work for them here, and you can take them back to the docks if I don't. Okay, Steelhart?"

"I don't like being lied to," Steelhart growled.

"Nobody does," Collins said, "but it's not a federal crime, either. You can't go throwing people in the drink every time they do something you don't like."

Steelhart gave Collins a nasty look but said nothing else. He stormed off and disappeared through a hatchway, while the crewmen returned to their work with the barrels.

"Thanks for saving us," Frank said.

"Yeah," Joe said. "It's a long swim back to Bayport."

"Don't thank me yet," Collins said. "You two have some explaining to do. Why did you tell Steelhart that I wanted to see you?"

"Like we said," Frank told him, "we're looking for jobs."

"What kind of jobs?" Collins asked.

"Radio jobs," Joe said. "We want to be radio announcers."

Collins laughed. "And what gives you the idea that you can find a radio job out here in the middle of the ocean? Most people look for radio work on dry land."

"Keith Wyatt told us that you were running a pirate station out here," Frank said.

Collins's expression became more serious. "Wyatt, eh? Well, I did ask him if he knew anybody who might want to work for Skull and Bones. I'd hoped he'd give me a little advance warning before sending somebody to see me, though."

"We just couldn't wait," Joe said. "You know how it is."

"Well," Collins said sympathetically, "I guess I do. I was a young radio announcer once myself. In fact, I'm not that old *yet*. I know what it's like to want to get your hands on that microphone right away."

He paused, studying the Hardys, then said, "Tell you what, I'll take you belowdecks, show you the equipment, and give you an audition. But first——"

Collins turned in the direction Steelhart had gone. "Hey, Captain!" he shouted. "Don't forget that you've got another passenger to pick up in a half hour. And a lot more fuel barrels to bring back from the warehouse."

After a moment Steelhart threw open the hatch and stomped out, resolutely ignoring Collins. Then he lowered himself over the railing and climbed back down to the tugboat. Frank noticed that Collins had a dark look on his face as he watched Steelhart go.

"That old man's been nothing but trouble," Collins said. "I don't think he's got all his marbles intact, if you know what I mean. One of these days he's *really* going to fly off the handle, and something awful's gonna happen."

"Why don't you get rid of him?" Joe asked.

"I'd love to," Collins said, "but he owns this ship. If he didn't, I'd ask J.R. to get rid of him so fast it would make your head spin."

"J.R.?" Frank asked.

"Jolly Roger, the owner of the station," Collins said. "Come on, boys, follow me."

Collins opened a hatch and gestured the Hardys

54

inside. Frank and Joe stepped through into the dimly lit passageway beyond.

It took Frank's eyes a moment to adjust to the darkness, but when they did he saw that he and Joe were in a narrow passage leading to a flight of stairs. Collins walked ahead of them, led them down a level, and opened a hatchway into a cramped cabin.

Frank stepped inside and looked around. The cabin appeared to be a nautical version of the radio studio where Joe worked back at WBBX. The electronic components looked older, and electrical wires snaked around the floor where somebody might trip over them, but all the necessary equipment seemed to be there. There was a console similar to the one at WBBX, with a pair of CD players and a tape deck mounted on top. There was even a turntable.

"As you can see," Collins said, "we have all the amenities. Skull and Bones is a real radio station, even if we lack a couple of technical requirements, like an FCC license." He settled into the swivel chair that sat in front of the console. "So," he asked, "have you boys worked in radio before?"

"Uh, well," Joe said, "I was a disc jockey at my, um, high school radio station. So I've got lots of experience."

"See, we had this act going," Frank explained. "We called ourselves Big Brother and the Renegade Kid."

Concealing a grin, Joe looked over at his brother approvingly. Frank was thinking fast, coming up with aliases so that Collins, or anybody else involved

55

who might hear them on the air, wouldn't know who they were.

"Yeah, we're the Smith brothers," Joe said. "I'm the Kid, and he's Big Bro."

"I see," Collins said, a dubious look on his face. "Ordinarily, those wouldn't exactly be glowing résumés. However, we are a little short on talent at the moment. In fact, I'm the only announcer we have. Of course, I expect that situation to turn around any time now since our reputation is growing."

Collins paused, sizing up the boys, then said, "I'd be willing to let you guys work here for the time being. If I like your work, I might even let you stay. But you'll have to pass the audition first."

"Sounds fair," Joe said. "What do we have to do?"

"Each of you will do a half-hour shift, right now, while I listen," Collins said. "At the end of the two shifts, I'll decide whether one or both of you gets the job. Who wants to go first?"

"I will," Joe said. "Where should I sit?"

"Right here," Collins said, rising from the swivel chair. "I'll go to my office down the hall and listen to you. See you in an hour."

Joe studied the equipment for a moment and chose some CDs to play. Then he flicked a switch and, using his new deejay name, started broadcasting. He was careful to vary his tone and style enough from his WBBX show that listeners wouldn't recognize him. At the end of the half hour Frank took over. With Joe sitting beside him and showing him what switches to throw and knobs to turn, Frank managed to get through his half hour in fairly good form.

Joe wondered what the response at BBX would be to the new pirate deejays. Frank was wondering if they had knocked Chet off the air with their own program. Frank had to admit he found that a little amusing and was just about to tune in to BBX to see if Chet was on the air when the door to the studio opened.

"Congratulations!" Collins cried, his black eyes shining. "You've both got the job!"

"Great," Joe said. "When do we start?"

"Tomorrow afternoon would be fine," Collins said. "We're starting out with small shifts until we start broadcasting full-time. The Kid can take the ten A.M. to noon shift, and Big Brother can go from noon to two P.M. How's that sound?"

"Just fine," Frank said. "Only, how do we get back and forth from the shore? We don't have to live on board this ship, do we?"

"Why not?" Collins asked. "I do." Then he laughed. "Just kidding, guys. Steelhart will pick you up tomorrow morning at nine and take you back at two."

"I thought you just told us that Steelhart is an unreliable madman," Frank said.

"I did," Collins said. "But he's the best we've got. And he's being paid good money by J.R. to help out around the station. So he'll do what I tell him to do. In fact, you can tell him that I said he should take you back to Bayport right now. Go on up topside

57

while I take care of business down here. Steelhart should be back from his last trip to Bayport by now."

Frank and Joe left the cramped cabin the way they'd come in, climbing up the narrow stairs and exiting through the hatch. As he blinked his eyes in the bright sunlight, Frank didn't at first recognize the figure that was standing directly in front of him on the other side of the hatch.

"You!" shouted the figure, stepping back as though startled.

Frank shaded his eyes with one hand. The dark figure suddenly became recognizable.

"Keith Wyatt!" Frank exclaimed.

"Frank and Joe Hardy!" Wyatt exclaimed in turn.

Wyatt cupped his hands around his mouth and yelled through the open hatchway behind the Hardys, "Hey, Collins! Better get up here! You've got a pair of spies on board your ship!"

7 A Trap for Jolly Roger

Joe slammed the hatch hastily behind himself before Collins could hear Wyatt's accusations.

"Keep it quiet," Frank hissed, seeing that Wyatt was about to yell another warning to Collins.

"Yeah," Joe said. "What did we do to deserve this?"

"What did you do?" Wyatt roared. "You accused me of throwing a hand grenade through Bill Crandall's window. You came into the Seven-Thirty Club looking for a fight. And now you turn up on the S.S. *Marconi*. I can't get rid of you guys."

"Okay, okay," Frank said. "We're sorry we said those things. Let's call a truce, all right?"

"Yeah," Joe said. "Besides, what makes you think we're spies?"

"What else would you be doing here?" Wyatt asked. "You work for Crandall, right?"

Joe put on his most innocent face. "Not anymore," he said. "We quit that job. Now we're looking for work with Skull and Bones."

"Right," Frank said. "Joe and I wanted to work together at the same station, but Crandall wouldn't give me a spot at WBBX. So we came here instead."

"I think I'm gonna be sick," Wyatt said, looking at the Hardys with disgust. He stared at the brothers through narrowed eyes. "I'm not sure I buy this. Why would you leave a cushy job at WBBX to come to a floating junkbin like this?"

"Like Frank said," Joe told him, "we wanted to work together. We thought a brother broadcasting team would drum up great publicity for the station. WBBX didn't buy it, but Skull and Bones did."

"Well, you guys do what you want," Wyatt said. "I've got a job interview with Jimmy Collins."

"Wait a minute," Joe said. "You told us yesterday that you weren't interested in working at Skull and Bones."

"That was yesterday," Wyatt said. "I changed my mind. It's not like I can get work anywhere else, you know? I'm three weeks late on my rent, so if I don't get a job here, I'm going to end up out on the street."

Wyatt elbowed his way past the Hardys and opened up the hatch. "Now, if you don't mind, I'm going to talk to Jimmy Collins."

"I hope you don't mention any of that spy stuff to

him," Joe said. "Or that we used to work for WBBX."

"Yeah," Frank said. "We'd like to keep our jobs here. So if you just don't say anything to Collins about us, it'll make life a lot easier. And if you need any favors, just ask us." Frank told Wyatt about the deejay names he and Joe were using and asked Wyatt not to reveal their true names.

Wyatt thought about it for a moment. "Maybe I will, maybe I won't," he said finally. "You guys don't give me any more trouble, I'll seriously think about keeping my mouth shut. Deal?"

"Deal," Frank and Joe said.

As soon as Wyatt closed the door and disappeared into the passageway, Joe collapsed against a bulkhead with relief. "Whew!" he gasped. "That was a close one."

"*Too* close," Frank said. "We still don't know if we can trust Wyatt to keep quiet around Collins."

"Yeah," Joe said, "but we don't have any choice. We just have to keep our fingers crossed that Wyatt doesn't get mad at us again and open his big mouth."

Steelhart, who had been loading more fuel barrels on board the ship, approached the Hardys, who eyed him warily. He gruffly told them to get on the tugboat, and they climbed down. Without speaking to the brothers again, Steelhart sealed himself away in the small cabin and piloted the small craft back toward Barmet Bay. As they leaned against the rear of the tug, Frank and Joe considered what they should do next.

"Well, we've found the pirate station," Joe said. "Maybe that's enough."

"Right," Frank said. "Crandall said there's a branch office of the FCC near Bayport. We'll call him when we get to shore so that he can have one of the FCC guys waiting when we get back. Then we can tell them where the pirate station is."

"And they can go close it down," Joe added.

Frank suddenly frowned. "Why do I have a feeling it's not going to turn out to be that simple?"

"Don't worry so much," Joe said. "You should—" Suddenly he slapped the side of his head with the palm of his hand.

"Oh, no!" Joe exclaimed. "I almost forgot. I'm late for my shift at BBX. Crandall's gonna kill me! This is the worst thing a radio announcer can do. It's what got Keith Wyatt fired in the first place."

"I wouldn't sweat it," Frank told him. "I told Crandall that you'd probably have trouble keeping up with your schedule, so we found a substitute for you."

"A substitute?" Joe repeated. "You mean you found somebody who could actually replace Joltin' Joe Hardy? Who is this genius of the airwaves?"

"Chet Morton," Frank said, trying to keep a straight face.

Joe's eyes went wide. "Unbelievable! Now BBX is really in trouble."

"And that's a classic single by Meatwood Flack . . . I mean Feetwood Hack . . . I mean . . .

what was the name of that group again?" Chet's voice boomed out of the speaker in Crandall's office, where Joe and Frank were talking to Crandall and a man from the FCC. "Well, never mind. Here's another record I'm sure you'll like," Chet said finally. "If, um, I can just remember what button to push to make it play."

Joe groaned. "If Chet sits in on my show much longer, he'll do more damage to BBX than Skull and Bones Radio could ever do."

Bill Crandall, seated behind his desk, leaned back in his chair. "The damage has already been done. Skull and Bones jammed our signal for more than two hours today. You boys were terrific, by the way."

"Thanks," Joe said. "Collins thought so, too—he hired us on the spot."

"We'll have to do something fast," Crandall said. "Our sponsors have already started to withdraw their commercials. If this keeps up much longer, we'll be forced to close down the station."

"But it *won't* keep up much longer, right?" Frank said. "Now that we've discovered where the pirate radio station is located, the FCC can close it down, right?"

"Unfortunately, no," said a tall, thin man leaning against Crandall's desk. John Kitchener was about sixty years old, with salt and pepper hair and ruggedly handsome features. He wore an expensive-looking gray suit with a perfectly knotted silk tie. "According to what you've told me, they've an-

63

chored the station in international waters. The FCC has no jurisdiction there."

"Then who does?" Joe asked.

"There are treaties that govern radio broadcasts in international waters," Kitchener said. "There was a case a few years back of a station broadcasting in international waters outside New York City."

"What happened?" Frank asked. "Was the FCC able to close them down?"

"No," Kitchener said. "But eventually the Coast Guard was. It's a tricky business, though, and there's a lot of red tape involved. We can't move on the station right away. Besides, I'm not sure this is the right time to make a move on them."

"Why not?" Joe asked.

"This is an unusual case," Kitchener said. "Most pirate stations are simply interested in broadcasting without government supervision. But from what you've told me, Collins doesn't seem to be the major force behind the station. This J.R. — Jolly Roger, as he calls himself — is the station's owner. And J.R. doesn't seem to be interested in just broadcasting. It looks as though he wants revenge on WBBX."

"That's true," Joe said. "Why else would he be broadcasting on WBBX's frequency?"

"And why else would he have the radio announcers make threats against WBBX on the air?" Frank said.

"Not to mention the threatening letters," said

Crandall, "or the phony hand grenade or the electric shock to Joe."

"Well, we're not certain that the electric shock is related to the other things," Frank said, "though it wouldn't surprise me."

"So it's my guess," Kitchener said, "that if the Coast Guard closes down Skull and Bones Radio without catching this Jolly Roger fellow, he might turn around and start another station in the same area, also broadcasting on WBBX's frequency. And the next one will be even harder to find than this one."

"Oh, great," Crandall moaned. "And before you know it there won't be any WBBX left at all."

"Right," Kitchener said. "So we have to catch this Jolly Roger fellow now. If we mount an all-out assault on Skull and Bones without knowing where J.R. is, we just drive him deeper underground—or should I say underwater? What we need is somebody who can go undercover and smoke him out before he knows that we're on to him."

"I suppose you'll use FCC agents for that job," Joe said, a hint of disappointment in his voice.

"I was thinking more in terms of using you two boys," Kitchener said. "You've already infiltrated Skull and Bones. You seem to have won the trust of the station manager. And from what I've heard of your reputation as local detectives, you're probably as good at this kind of thing as anybody we've got at the FCC."

Joe perked up. "We just got lucky a few times," he said.

"Shut up," Frank said, "or he might think you mean it."

"Don't worry," Kitchener assured them. "I want you boys to head back out to Skull and Bones tomorrow and begin your job. Find out as much as you can about Jolly Roger and report back to me."

"Right, sir," Joe said. "We will."

Kitchener shook hands with the Hardys and Crandall and then left. Before they stepped out of Crandall's office, Joe turned toward the speaker on Crandall's wall and listened for a moment to Chet.

"Here's one of my favorite commercials," Chet was saying. "And I'm sure it's one of your favorites, too. I'm going to play it any second now, as soon as I remember where I put it."

"I don't think I can take much more of this," Joe said, turning to leave.

Suddenly Chet began making a gasping noise on the air. "Wait . . . wait a minute," Chet sputtered. "Something's wrong . . . I . . . I . . ."

There were some coughing and choking sounds, followed by a thudding noise. Then there was dead silence.

"Something's happened to Chet!" Joe shouted.

8 Bill of Sale

Frank dashed into the studio just ahead of Joe and found Chet facedown on the console. Suddenly Frank began coughing violently as he noticed a noxious odor in the studio.

Joe was overcome by the foul-smelling fumes, too, and between coughs he said to his brother, "Let's get Chet out of here." First Joe took a large envelope that was sitting on Chet's lap and quickly tossed it out into the hallway. Joe pressed a button to start another CD playing, then he and Frank dragged Chet as gently as possible into the hall.

"Um, uh, what's goin' on?" Chet mumbled as he propped himself up in a sitting position against the wall.

"That's what we're wondering," Frank said. "Are you okay, Chet?"

"Okay?" Chet asked. "Oh, uh, yeah, I . . ." His eyes popped open, and he shook his head. All at once he started coughing violently.

"I guess he's not okay," Joe said. "What's this package that was on your lap? It smells awfully nasty," Joe said. "There was some kind of gas inside it or something."

"Gas?" Chet tried to sit up straighter. "Yeah, I . . . I thought I smelled something funny, and I, um . . ."

"Take your time, Chet," Frank said. "There must have been a gas bomb in this package." The large brown envelope had been stapled on top. Inside was a thick plastic bag that had a pull tab on it.

"When you ripped open the envelope, Chet, you pulled open the tab. The friction caused the bomb to ignite," Frank explained. "That produced the gas cloud. Now there are only ashes inside the package."

While Frank and Joe tended to Chet, station personnel were running frantically around the offices, opening windows and propping fans outside the studio door to draw the toxic fumes out. Bill Crandall reassured everyone that there was no serious fire, and that the odor was just a prank gas bomb that Chet had received.

Joe held his breath and dashed into the studio to see if everything was in order. Chet had another CD in place in the machine, so all Joe had to do was press a button to start it playing. Then Joe went back out to see how Chet was doing.

Chet was standing up, and the color had returned to his face. "I'm okay," Chet was saying when Joe was back at his side. "I could use a soda or a snack, though."

The Hardys knew Chet was back to his normal self since he was thinking about food again.

"There's only a slight odor left in there," Joe said. He took a handkerchief from his pocket and gingerly lifted the envelope. "It's addressed to Chet in care of the station, from 'An Admirer.'"

"How could Chet have an admirer already?" Frank asked. "He only started doing the show today."

"Yeah," Joe said. "I've been at the station for four weeks, and I haven't gotten a single package yet from an admirer."

"Where did you get the package, Chet?" Frank asked.

"Jack Ruiz dropped it off," Chet said. "I don't know where he got it from."

"Jack Ruiz?" Joe asked. "The same guy you saw in the studio before I almost got electrocuted yesterday?"

"One and the same," Chet said. "You don't think there's a connection, do you?"

"I don't know," Joe said, "but I think we'd better have a little talk with Mr. Ruiz before we leave this afternoon."

"Are you okay, Chet?" Frank asked, walking with his friend back toward the swivel chair inside the studio. "Can you finish the show?"

"Yeah, I think so," Chet said.

"Then Joe and I are going to have a talk with Jack Ruiz," Frank said, leaving the studio.

Ruiz's office was next to Crandall's. Frank and Joe paused outside the studio for a moment, thinking about what they would say.

"What should we ask him?" Joe said. "We can't come right out and tell him we think he's connected with this Skull and Bones business."

"We'll just ask him some innocent questions," Frank said. "Try and see if he might have some motivation for harming his own radio station."

As they approached the door of Ruiz's office, they heard loud voices inside. Frank recognized Jack Ruiz's voice, but not the other. He looked quizzically at Joe.

"Charles Horwitz," Joe whispered back. "He's the other co-owner of the station."

Instead of knocking on the door, the Hardys paused for a moment and listened. The voices were so loud that they could be plainly understood from where the brothers were standing in the hallway.

"I think you're being an idiot, as usual," Ruiz was saying, an angry edge to his voice. "But that won't stop me from taking advantage of your stupidity."

"You'd never dream of making things easy for me, would you, Jack?" Horwitz said. "Sometimes I'm sorry I ever agreed to become your partner."

70

"The feeling is mutual," Ruiz said. "But that won't matter much longer, will it?"

"I guess not," Horwitz said. "I'll see you later."

The door popped open, and a well-tanned man in his late fifties came out, apparently Charles Horwitz. The Hardys backed off quickly, pretending that they were just walking down the hallway and not eavesdropping. But Horwitz paid no attention to them as he headed down the hall to another office.

When Horwitz was gone, the Hardys approached Ruiz's door again. Frank knocked twice, and a deep voice from inside told them to enter. They stepped into the office to find Jack Ruiz sitting behind his desk. His office looked like a slightly less cluttered version of Bill Crandall's. Ruiz seemed to be absorbed in signing some papers, but he looked up as the brothers entered.

"Oh, hello, Joe," Ruiz said. "Is this your brother, whom I've been hearing so much about from Bill Crandall?"

"That's right," Joe said. "I guess you two haven't met yet."

"I met you briefly in Mr. Crandall's office yesterday," Frank said, "but we really weren't introduced."

"So what can I do for you boys?" Ruiz asked. "Bill tells me that you're helping out somehow with this pirate radio thing."

"That's correct, sir," Frank said. "He asked us to keep our eyes open around the station, see what we can find."

"And have you found anything yet?" Ruiz asked.

Frank looked at Joe before answering. He wondered if they should tell Ruiz that they had infiltrated the pirate radio station, but decided that they better not. If Ruiz had anything to do with Skull and Bones, letting him know that they had gotten jobs as deejays there might put them in jeopardy. Of course, Collins may have told him about the new deejays he hired, but they had used phony names, so they should be safe.

"We've talked with some people," Frank said. "Asked a few questions."

"Yeah," said Joe, who seemed to have come to the same conclusion as Frank. "We've gotten a few leads, but they haven't led us very far yet."

"What we were wondering," Frank said, "was whether you had any idea why somebody would want to hurt WBBX. It sure looks as though this Jolly Roger guy is trying to drive you off the air, but nobody seems to know why."

"I'm afraid I don't know any more than anyone else," Ruiz said, "and, in fact, it will soon no longer concern me."

"What do you mean?" Joe asked. "You're co-owner of the station, right? I'd think you'd be pretty concerned about its future."

A look of chagrin crossed Ruiz's face. "I shouldn't have said that," he told them. "Of course I'm concerned about the future of the station. But I don't know any more about Skull and Bones Radio than anyone else around here does. So, if you'll excuse me, I have some business to take care of."

"Just one more question, sir?" Frank said.

"Yes?" Ruiz said impatiently.

"Chet said that you brought a package into the studio a few minutes ago," Frank continued. "Do you know where that came from?"

"I found it on my desk," Ruiz said. "I have no idea how it got there."

Ruiz turned back to his work, making it clear that the Hardys were expected to leave. Frank and his brother exchanged puzzled glances, then slipped back out into the hallway.

"That was interesting," Frank said. "Wonder why he's not worried about Skull and Bones?"

"Even more important," Joe said, "why doesn't he *tell* us why he's not worried about Skull and Bones?"

"That's awfully suspicious, all right," Frank said.

Joe's eyes opened wide. "Hey, I just thought of something else. Jimmy Collins kept referring to Jolly Roger as J.R., right?"

"Right," Frank agree. "So what?"

"So what are Ruiz's initials?" Joe asked.

Frank's face broke out in a big grin. "I didn't even think of that. Good work, bro!"

"I think we'd better ask some more questions about Jack Ruiz," Joe said. "Don't you?"

"Agreed," Frank said, "but we'll have to ask somebody else besides Jack Ruiz."

"Where's Charles Horwitz's office?" Frank asked.

73

"Right down here," Joe said, pointing down the hall. "Want to stop by for a visit?"

"Lead on," Frank told him.

Charles Horwitz was an attractive man with stunning silver hair. Watching him lean back in his chair, legs crossed, Frank thought that he looked like the kind of man who truly enjoyed his work. He wore an expensive-looking gray suit, and there always seemed to be a slight smile on his lips.

After introducing themselves, the Hardys asked Horwitz if he knew anything about the pirate station.

"No," Horwitz said. "I'm afraid I don't know any more about this Skull and Bones business than you do. Probably less, if you kids are the sharp detectives Bill Crandall says you are."

"Could you tell us a few things about this station?" Frank asked. "Maybe that'll help us understand why Jolly Roger is so anxious to hurt you."

"I'll tell you what I can," Horwitz said. "I guess I'm something of an expert on this station. Jack Ruiz and I have been here since the beginning, twenty years ago."

"Where'd you meet Mr. Ruiz?" Joe asked. "Are you old friends?"

"Well, not in the social sense," Horwitz said. "Jack and I are business partners and have been for a long time."

"Has there ever been any trouble between the two of you?" Frank asked.

"Trouble?" Horwitz asked, as though he were a

little puzzled by the question. "I'm not sure what you mean by that."

"Have there ever been any arguments between you, that sort of thing?" Joe asked.

"To be honest," Horwitz said, "Jack has always been a little jealous of my share of the station. He feels it cuts into his profits." Horwitz looked suddenly regretful at having spoken. "I really shouldn't be telling you this. Listen, boys, I'd like to help out, but my business relationship with Jack Ruiz isn't something I can talk about freely. I hope you understand."

"Sure," Joe said. "Sorry if we bothered you."

"That's okay," Horwitz said. "You're on our side. I hope you catch those Skull and Bones people and do the rest of us here at WBBX proud."

After leaving Horwitz's office, Frank and Joe wandered back down to the studio. Chet, having recovered from his experience with the gas bomb, was going through a stack of CDs.

Joe picked up the package that had contained the bomb and examined it. The package bore the words "To Chet, from an admirer" inscribed in pen.

"Maybe we should check Ruiz's handwriting," Joe suggested. "See if it matches what's on this package."

"Okay," Frank said, "but where can we find a sample of it?"

"Maybe on the bulletin board," Joe said, indicating a board on the studio wall covered with small slips of paper. After examining it, however, neither

Frank nor Joe could find anything that had been obviously handwritten by Ruiz. Most of the notes were typed.

"Guess we'll have to check his office," Frank said finally. "Think he's still around?"

"We can take a look," Joe said.

Nobody answered this time when Frank rapped on Jack Ruiz's door. Frank slowly turned the handle and opened the door. He peered into the room. No one was there.

"I don't suppose Mr. Ruiz would mind if we just took a quick look around," Frank said.

"Hey, I can't see why he would," Joe said with a smile. "Let's go inside."

Frank pushed the door the rest of the way open and stepped inside. The light was out, and the desk had been cleaned up.

"Do you think he's gone for the day?" Frank suggested.

"Maybe," Joe said. "It's not that late, though. He may have just stepped out."

The papers that Ruiz had been working on earlier were neatly stacked in the middle of the desk. Frank picked one up and examined it.

"It looks like a bill of sale," Frank said.

"A bill of sale?" Joe asked. "For what?"

Frank skimmed the fine print that covered most of the page. "I'm not sure," he said, "but it looks like—holy cow! This is a bill of sale for the station. For WBBX."

"You're kidding!" Joe cried, snatching the paper

from Frank's hand. "Why would he be selling the station?"

"Can you blame him?" Frank said. "Maybe he's getting out while the getting's good, before Jolly Roger ruins his business."

"Right," Joe said, "but what kind of sucker would buy the station at this point?"

"Maybe somebody who doesn't know about the pirate station," Frank suggested. "Whose signature is on that piece of paper?"

"Nobody's, yet," Joe said. "But there's space for two signatures. And I bet one of them will be Ruiz's."

"If Ruiz is selling the station," Frank asked, "why would he try to sabotage it with a pirate station at the same time?"

"Maybe it's some kind of scam," Joe said. "Sell the station for a bundle, sabotage it with the pirate station, then buy it back cheap."

"That's a thought," Frank said. "But if that's his plan, the timing is a little off. Why not wait a few days to unleash Jolly Roger and his team of merry disc jockeys?"

"I don't know," Joe said. "Maybe that's why Skull and Bones is only broadcasting part-time now. Maybe he's really going to zap WBBX when the sale is complete."

"Maybe," Frank said. "Hey, do you still have that package? Why don't you compare the handwriting on it with Ruiz's signature on one of these other papers?"

77

"Good idea," Joe said, holding up the package he had taken from the radio studio. He then found a letter on the desk that bore Ruiz's signature. The address on the front of the package was written in a different color ink and in a different style of script from the signature, but it was hard to tell if it was or wasn't Ruiz's handwriting.

"Of course," Frank said, "some people's signatures are very different from their regular writing, so it's hard to be sure."

There was a sound from the hallway. Frank looked up, startled.

"We'd better get out of here," he said, "before somebody catches us snooping around in Ruiz's office."

"Okay," Joe said, "but I'll hang on to this package until we get another chance to compare it with Jack Ruiz's handwriting."

The Hardys slipped out of Ruiz's office, then continued down the hallway and out the front door of the building. Joe tore the label off the package and slipped it into his wallet, which he then put back in his pocket. He then put the remainder of the package under his arm, so they could examine it later.

"I guess that's all we can do around the station for now," Frank said. "We'd better get moving."

"That's fine with me," Joe said.

The brothers climbed into their van, which was parked at the curb in front of the station. Frank buckled his seat belt and gunned the engine as Joe settled in on the passenger side. It was midafternoon, and traffic on Bayport's streets was getting heavy.

"So what do you think about Ruiz?" Frank asked his brother.

"I don't know what to think," Joe said. "He's probably got the money and the knowledge to run a pirate station, but I'm still not sure what his motive is. Maybe we should—"

Suddenly there was an exploding sound. Frank felt the steering wheel yank itself out of his grip.

"I think we blew a tire!" he shouted.

"Can't you slow down?" Joe asked, gripping the dashboard.

Before Frank could wrestle the steering wheel back under control, the van swerved into the left-hand lane, directly into the path of an oncoming car.

9 Rendezvous in the Bay

Heart pounding, Frank fought for control of the van, but the wheel kept pulling to the left, directly into the path of the car.

"Turn to the right!" Joe shouted. "Fast!"

"I'm trying," Frank cried in return, "but the wheel won't turn."

Instead of turning back into the right lane, Frank yanked the wheel as hard as he could in the opposite direction, toward the left-hand side of the road.

"What are you doing?" Joe yelled at his brother. "Are you crazy?"

Frank didn't answer. Fortunately, the driver of the oncoming car saw what he was trying to do. The driver steered his vehicle into the lane that the

Hardys had just swerved out of. The van passed the car on the left, within a hair's breadth of its fender. Finally Frank brought the van to a screeching halt, right in the middle of the oncoming lane. Another car also squealed to a stop next to them. The driver leaned angrily on his horn, waving a fist out the window.

"Sorry," Frank said, trying to catch his breath. "I did the best I could."

"Whew!" Joe sank back into his seat. "I didn't even have time to buckle my seat belt."

"Next time do it before we pull out of the parking place," Frank said. He pushed open his door and climbed out into the street. The front left tire of the van was completely blown. Joe and Frank exchanged looks of frustration, then pushed the van out of the way of traffic.

It took them fifteen minutes to replace the blown tire with a spare from the rear of the van. When they were done, Joe picked up the damaged tire and began to examine it.

"This wasn't an accidental blowout," he said, pointing to slash marks in the rubber tread. "Somebody tampered with this tire while we were in the WBBX building."

"Why wasn't it flat when we came out?" Frank asked. "I would have noticed when I climbed into the driver's seat."

"They probably slashed it just enough so that it would blow when we started driving," Joe suggested.

81

"Which means that they weren't just trying to give us a hard time," Frank said.

"Right," Joe said. "They wanted us to have an accident. Somebody was trying to knock us off the Skull and Bones case—the hard way."

"Well," Frank said, "that makes me more determined than ever to solve the case."

Jimmy Collins wasn't expecting the brothers back at Skull and Bones until the next morning at ten. The Hardys had the rest of the evening to check on other aspects of the case. After changing the sabotaged tire, they decided to head to the local library, to check out a few facts that had been bothering them.

"For instance," Joe said as they entered the Bayport library, "who owns that warehouse down at the docks? Apparently, that's where Steelhart has been getting those large barrels of fuel that he takes out to the S.S. *Marconi*. But I doubt that Steelhart owns it himself, or Jimmy Collins."

"But it *may* belong to this mysterious J.R.," Frank said, walking up to the information desk. A young woman sat at the desk reading a paperback book.

"Excuse me, ma'am," Joe said. "We're wondering if you keep municipal records here. Documents that would show who owns various properties around the Bayport area."

The woman looked up from her book and smiled. "Yes, we do have a special Bayport section in the rear of the library. The librarian there can show you the microfiche file."

82

The librarian in the Bayport section was an elderly man who presided over cabinet after cabinet of microfilm and microfiche. At the Hardys' request he pulled out one tiny black microfiche from the thousands that seemed to fill the cabinets.

"I wonder how he knew this was the right one?" Joe asked. "I could never find anything in this place."

"Ours is not to question why," Frank said, sitting at a microfiche reader. "Let's just see what it says."

Frank switched on the light and slid the microfiche under the glass plate. A white and blue image appeared on the screen, the rows and columns of information shifting around as Frank adjusted the settings.

"Ah, here we go," Frank said. "Bayside Warehouse. Built 1978. Present Owner, Benjamin Harness of Harness Enterprises."

"Benjamin Harness?" Joe said. "Never heard of him."

"Well, I guess we'll have to find out more about him," Frank said. He stood up and took the microfiche back to the desk. "Excuse me," he said to the librarian. "Where can I find a telephone directory?"

The librarian handed him a directory from behind the desk. Frank flipped through the pages until he found a listing for Harness Enterprises.

"It's on the other side of town," he told his brother. "Maybe we should pay him a visit. It's getting late, but we may still catch him."

The librarian suddenly looked up. "Did you say Harness?" the man said. "Ben Harness?"

"That's right," Joe said. "Have you heard of him?"

"Sure," the librarian said. "Used to be fairly well known in this town a few years back. Until he lost his radio station."

Frank felt his detective sense tingling. "Radio station? What radio station?"

"Don't remember the name of it," the old man said. "Wasn't really my type of music. Rock and roll, you know."

"Right, we know," Joe said. "You don't know what happened to the station, do you?"

"It just couldn't compete," the librarian told him. "There was another station in town that got better ratings."

"Would you, um, happen to remember the name of the other station?" Frank asked.

"I believe I do," said the librarian. "It was called WBBX."

Harness Enterprises was located on the top three floors of a building in the upper-crust section of Bayport. A sign in the lobby invited the Hardys to ride the elevator to the seventh floor if they wished to visit the Harness offices. When they stepped off the elevator, they found themselves facing a female receptionist in a gray suit.

As they walked out of the elevator and toward the receptionist's desk, something caught Frank's eye. On the wall behind the receptionist were several bright gold and platinum LPs. Beneath each one was a small plaque and a sign that read Harness Records.

"Excuse me," Frank said to the receptionist. "I thought Harness Enterprises was in the radio business."

"We used to be," the receptionist said, "but we've diversified. Harness Enterprises is now primarily involved in the recording industry."

"You make records?" Joe asked.

"That's what I just said," the receptionist agreed.

"We were hoping we could speak with Mr. Harness," Frank said. "Just for a few minutes."

"I'm sorry," the receptionist said, "but Mr. Harness isn't in the office right now."

"Oh, that's too bad," Joe said. "Do you know when he'll be back?"

"He'll be in tomorrow morning," the receptionist said. "However, it would be easier if you simply left your demo tapes here at the desk. I'll be sure to pass them on to Mr. Harness."

"Demo tapes?" Frank asked.

"That's right," the receptionist said. "You *are* aspiring young musicians looking for a record contract, aren't you?"

"Uh, well, no," Joe said. "We just needed to talk to Mr. Harness about something important."

"That's what they all say," the receptionist replied. "Mr. Harness never talks to musicians without hearing a demo tape first."

"But we're not—" Joe protested.

"Never mind," Frank said, pulling his brother

back toward the elevator. "We'll be back with some demo tapes later."

In the elevator Joe turned angrily toward his brother and said, "Why'd you pull me out? We've got to talk to Harness."

"I know," Frank said, "but we weren't getting anywhere. As long as she thinks we're a couple of kids with a band, we'll never get near Harness. I bet they get a dozen visitors like us every day."

"Well," Joe said, "we could come back with a demo tape."

"And she'll throw it in the trash can the minute we leave," Frank said. "Get real. We'll need a better way to slip past her than that."

"So what's your idea?" Joe asked.

"I don't know," Frank said. "Let's think about it overnight. In the meantime, I want to take another look at that warehouse on Bayside Drive."

Fifteen minutes later the Hardys pulled their van onto Bayside Drive. They climbed out and started walking toward the warehouse, then paused.

Frank looked out over the water. A familiar tugboat was chugging up to the pier.

"Steelhart's back," Frank said.

"And he's got somebody with him," Joe said. "Looks like Keith Wyatt."

"Let's get back in the van so they don't see us," Frank said. "I want to see what they're up to."

Steelhart moored the tugboat at the dock, then walked to the warehouse. He emerged with two fuel barrels on a dolly, which he wheeled across the street and into the tug. Wyatt, meanwhile, headed directly for a telephone booth and made a call. After talking on the phone for about five minutes, he began walking in the direction of the van. Frank and Joe slouched low in their seats until he had passed.

In the rearview mirror Frank could see Wyatt heading for a small marina about five hundred feet behind them. Several dozen small boats were moored at the piers.

"Wonder what he's going there for?" Joe asked.

"Maybe he wants to take a boat ride," Frank said. "Let's follow him and see."

The Hardys slipped out of the van and quietly followed Keith Wyatt into the marina. Frank watched him walk up to a booth next to one of the piers. Wyatt handed some money to the man inside, then walked to a small motorboat and climbed in.

"He's renting a boat," Frank said. "I wonder where he's going."

"There's only one way to find out," Joe said. "Let's rent one, too."

Frank handed the man at the rental booth a cash deposit, and the man handed him a key in return. He pointed to a small boat next to the one that Wyatt had rented. By this time, Wyatt was already guiding his boat into Barmet Bay.

"We'd better move fast," Joe said, "before he loses us."

"How's he going to lose us in the middle of Barmet Bay?" Frank asked. "There aren't a lot of places to hide out there."

"That's true," Joe said. "And at least there are enough boats out today that we can blend into the crowd."

The brothers climbed into the small boat, and Frank pulled the chain on the outboard motor. The boat roared to life, and Joe steered it in the direction Wyatt had gone.

Wyatt headed straight into the middle of Barmet Bay, finally coming to a small island. He stopped the boat a few feet from shore, then took off his shoes and rolled up his pants legs. He stepped out of the boat and pulled it after him until it was securely grounded and couldn't float away. Finally he walked barefoot onto the island.

Joe cut the motor on their boat so that it drifted far enough away not to be noticed.

Another man appeared from the small patch of trees in the center of the island. He was about forty years old, with curly brown hair. He wore a black suit and a tie, but he was also barefoot. He spoke with Wyatt for about fifteen minutes, then they shook hands. Wyatt returned to his boat, and the man stepped back into the woods.

"Which one should we follow now?" Joe asked. "Wyatt or that other guy?"

"Let's follow the other guy," Frank said. "We can always track Wyatt down later, but we don't even know who that other guy is."

As Wyatt started back toward shore, the Hardys circled the tiny island in their motorboat until they saw the man in the black suit climb into a boat of his own and head back toward shore.

"Let's see where he goes," Frank said. He revved up the motor, and Joe guided it after the stranger.

Unfortunately, the man looked back and saw that he was being followed. Clearly disturbed, he gunned his own motor and raced off.

"He's going to give us a chase!" Joe cried.

"Well, we'll just have to give him a run for his money," Frank said, turning the outboard motor up to full throttle.

"Yeah," Joe said, "if this boat can keep up with him."

Unfortunately, it couldn't. The stranger's boat disappeared quickly around the island, and by the time the Hardys reached the other side of the island themselves, he was out of sight.

"So much for a wild boat chase," Joe said. "Next time, let's rent the high-priced boat, okay?"

"Hey, nobody warned me we were going to need anything faster than the one Wyatt rented," Frank complained.

Joe steered the boat back toward the marina. As they neared their destination, however, Frank suddenly noticed something farther down the shore.

"Hey, isn't that the boat we were just following?" he said, pointing to a motorboat moored to a private dock.

"I think you're right," Joe said. "Let's check it out."

There was nobody in sight at the private dock, so the Hardys pulled their own boat up to it and tied it to a convenient post. Then they climbed out and walked up to the shore.

"This looks like somebody's private land," Frank said, glancing at a fence surrounding a large parcel of waterfront property.

"It must belong to somebody *very* rich," Joe said. "There sure is a lot of land here."

A path led through thick woods, which were growing dark as the sun drew close to the horizon. The Hardys hesitated for a moment, then started walking up the path.

Frank noticed a sign that read Private: No Trespassing next to the road. "Do you suppose that means us?" he asked with a grin.

"Nah," Joe said. "That's just to keep the riffraff out."

Frank squinted into the woods. The outline of a large house was visible in the distance.

"Somebody does live up here," Frank said. "And, judging from the size of that house, you were right when you said that somebody was rich."

Suddenly there was a rustling noise in the shrubbery along the sides of the path. Before they could turn, both Frank and Joe felt someone grab their arms and pin them behind their backs.

"Take one more step, kids," a voice said from behind Frank, "and we'll snap your arms clean off!"

10 Off the Case

Joe and Frank felt themselves being frisked with professional efficiency. When their assailants were satisfied that they weren't carrying any weapons, the Hardys were released. They then spun around to face their attackers.

What they saw were a pair of hulking men in suits. They had the look, thought Joe, of professional bodyguards. Anybody would think twice before attacking them—or before attacking anybody that they were guarding—yet they would blend nicely into a crowded public place if nobody paid too much attention to them.

The one on the right, who had longish black hair, crossed his arms in front of his chest and began asking questions. "So what are you kids doing here?" he asked. "Just snooping around?"

"That's right," Joe said. "We were out for a boat ride, and we were curious who lived here."

"You know what they say about curiosity and the cat," the other man said. He had brown hair cut short in an almost military style. "You might want to give that some thought next time you decide to snoop around."

Joe heard footsteps coming behind him, from the direction of the large house. Was it another bodyguard? No, it was the man they had seen earlier in the boat. The man walked up to the bodyguards, smiled at them in recognition of a job well done, and turned to the Hardys.

From a distance the man had looked like a well-dressed executive out for a motorboat cruise in Barmet Bay. Up close the Hardys saw that he was younger than they had at first thought, probably in his late twenties. Under his suit jacket he wore an open-collared shirt without a tie, unbuttoned to reveal a tanned and hairy chest. A gold chain dangled around his neck. He had a glowing smile, which revealed a set of even white teeth. Joe had a feeling that he used the smile often, whether he was in a good mood or not.

"So what brings you boys to my house on this beautiful evening?" he asked. Then a look of mild surprise crossed his face. "Say, I think I recognize you kids. You were following my motorboat out in the bay, weren't you?"

When neither Joe nor Frank replied, the man's smile gave way to a look of mild impatience. "Looks to me as if you were spying, weren't you? Now, what reason could you possibly have for being interested in what I was doing out on that island?"

"We wanted to see who Keith Wyatt was meeting with," Frank said finally.

"Oh," the man said, smiling again. "Are you friends of Keith?"

"You could say that," Joe said. "Sort of."

"Sort of friends, eh?" the man said. "Well, I've been friends with Keith for several years. We go way back together, since he first started working in the radio business. In fact, he started out at my station."

"You run a radio station?" Joe asked in surprise.

"I used to run a radio station," the man said, "but now I'm in the record business."

Frank's eyes went wide. "You wouldn't happen to be Benjamin Harness, would you?"

The man smiled broadly. "I see that my reputation is growing by leaps and bounds. I'm Ben Harness, all right. And obviously you're a pair of intelligent, knowledgeable young men, since you've heard of me."

"Actually," Joe said, "we've been wanting to talk with you."

"Well, now you've got your chance," Harness said. "Though if I were you, I'd find a different method of getting to see me next time. If the dogs had gotten to you before my bodyguards here, you might not have been in good enough shape to do any talking—if you get my drift."

"Er, yes," Frank said. "That's a pretty clear drift."

"So what was it you wanted to talk to me about?" Harness asked. "Although I'm enjoying this conversation immensely, I'm afraid I have pressing duties to which I will soon need to attend."

"Well," Joe said, "we heard that you owned a record company . . ."

"And," Frank said, picking up on Joe's line of patter, "we work for a new radio station called Skull and Bones Radio. Have you heard of it?"

"Yes," Harness said. "As a matter of fact, I already have."

"Well, anyway," Frank said, "we think it's great that you've got your own record company."

"Yeah," Joe said. "We've really been wanting to talk to you."

"And why is that?" Harness asked. "Is there something I can do for you?"

"There might be," Frank said. "You've got records to play and, well, we play records."

"So maybe we can reach some kind of deal with you," Joe said.

"Deal?" Harness asked. "You're not talking about something illegal, are you? Like playing my records if I give you a little money on the side?"

"Oh, no," Frank said hastily. "We'd never think of asking for something like that."

"Of course," Joe said, thinking quickly, "Keith Wyatt told us that he's got a deal like that with you."

The look on Harness's face told Joe that he'd struck a nerve. "Keith told you that, did he?" Harness said. "And why did Keith tell you such a thing?"

"I guess he was just feeling talkative," Joe said.

"Keith should learn to keep his mouth shut," Harness said, "if he knows what's good for him. I'll have you know that I've merely been encouraging Mr. Wyatt to play some of the new records from my company, Harness Records. We have some fine new talent, and we want them to receive exposure on radio stations like Skull and Bones."

"Is that why you were discussing it with Keith on an island in the middle of Barmet Bay?" Frank asked.

"Then you were spying on *Keith*," Harness said, "hoping to get on the payroll with him. I'll have you know that I was meeting Keith on that island because I like water. That's why my house is located on the bay. I thought it would be amusing to meet Mr. Wyatt in a scenic location. Now, do you boys have any more questions? If not, I—"

"As a matter of fact," Frank said, "we do have another question. It's about a piece of property that you own, on Bayside Drive. It's called the Bayside Warehouse."

"The Bayside Warehouse?" Harness repeated. "It sounds vaguely familiar."

"It's not far from here," Joe said, pointing back toward the docks. "According to the records at the library, you own it."

95

"That doesn't surprise me," Harness said. "I own a number of properties in the Bayport area. The radio and record businesses have their ups and downs, so I find it worthwhile to have some earnings from real estate to keep my cash flow in good shape."

"What is the warehouse used for?" Frank asked.

"No doubt I rent it to someone," Harness replied. "If I were using it for my own storage, I'm sure I would recognize the name."

"Who do you rent it to?" Joe asked.

"I have no idea," Harness said. "I'd have records of that in my office downtown, but I couldn't tell you off the top of my head."

"Then could we visit you at the office?" Joe asked.

"Sorry, boys," Harness said. "I'm afraid I just don't have the time. I'm a very busy man. Now, if you'll excuse me, I'll have my bodyguards escort you off the property."

"Can we ask one more question?" Frank asked.

"You boys are just full of questions, aren't you?" Harness said. Then he smiled. "You remind me of myself when I started in this business. Always looking for an opportunity or making contacts. All right, one last question, but make it quick."

"What happened to your radio station?" Frank asked. "Why did it go off the air?"

"The radio business is tough," Harness said. "Stations go off the air all the time."

"Was it poor ratings?" Joe asked.

"It's *always* poor ratings," Harness replied. "If

96

you don't have enough listeners, you can't get advertisers. And if you can't get advertisers, you don't have enough money to run the station. And if you don't have enough money to run the station, you can't get listeners. It's a vicious circle."

"And I guess BBX was stiff competition," Frank said.

Harness's smile disappeared. "I guess you could say that. They got better ratings than we did. Bayport is a small radio market. There's just not enough room for two stations playing the same kind of music."

"So how do you feel about BBX now?" Joe asked.

Harness snapped his fingers at his two bodyguards. "That's enough questions, boys," he said to Frank and Joe. "I'm out of here. Get on your boat and go home."

Joe started to protest, but the short-haired bodyguard grabbed him by the arm and pulled him forcibly down the path. The long-haired bodyguard did the same with Frank. Harness headed back toward his house. Moments later the Hardys found themselves back in their rented motorboat, heading toward the marina.

"I don't trust Harness one bit," Joe said as they pulled in to the slip next to the pier where they had picked up the boat. "It appears that he's involved in a payola scheme with Wyatt—paying Wyatt to play his records. I wonder what else Harness is scheming."

"You and me both," Frank said. "He sure has reason to hate BBX, and to want to blow it off the air."

"If Keith Wyatt got a job at Skull and Bones, then we'll see him tomorrow," Joe said. "We can ask him some questions about Harness."

"Right," Frank said. "Which reminds me. We start work tomorrow morning. So we'd better get home and get a good night's sleep. We want to impress our new boss, right?"

"This is Big Brother, and you're listening to Skull and Bones Radio, the station that's so exciting it's practically . . . illegal!" Removing his headset, Frank threw the switch that Joe had told him would turn off the microphone.

Frank turned around to face his brother, Joe, who had just finished his own shift in the cramped radio cabin of the S.S. *Marconi.* "So how am I doing, Joe? Think I'll ever be a big-time deejay?"

"Don't quit your day job," Joe suggested.

"This *is* my day job," Frank said. "But I won't drop out of school just yet."

"It's so strange knowing that we're broadcasting over WBBX's frequency—that we're doing something illegal," Joe said.

"I know," Frank told him. "Just keep in mind *why* we're doing it."

"I'm going to go topside while you're on the air and take a look around," Joe said.

"I already took a look around while you were

98

doing your shift," Frank said, pulling an LP out of the box next to the console. "It's a big ship, but there's nothing up there to indicate who's running this station."

"Well, at least I'll get some fresh air," Joe said. "Are you sure you can operate that console by yourself?"

"If you can do it, I can do it," Frank said. "See you later."

Joe pushed open the hatch, stepped into the hallway, and went up the stairs. It was midday and the sun was directly overhead. Steelhart was off in the tug again, and his crewmen were wrestling the fuel barrels around on the deck.

As far as Joe could tell, the fuel in the barrels was used to run the electric generators that powered the station. Apparently a lot of power was needed, because Steelhart was continually bringing more barrels from the warehouse. The crewmen periodically carried another barrel through a hatchway, beyond which Joe could hear a mechanical chugging sound.

When the crewmen saw Joe watching, they turned and made jeering comments at him. Joe got the impression that Steelhart and his crewmen didn't like the Skull and Bones personnel much. In fact, he had the feeling that they hated them.

Joe strolled around the deck for a while but saw nothing new. Finally, just as he was about to go belowdecks again, he saw Steelhart's tug approaching. Keith Wyatt was on board. Earlier, Jimmy Collins had mentioned that Wyatt had been hired to hold down the shift following Frank's. Steelhart must be bringing him in to do his show, Joe decided.

Wyatt climbed over the deck just ahead of Steelhart. Joe waved to him, and Wyatt walked over to him as Steelhart disappeared to some other part of the ship.

"Well, I see we're all employees of Skull and Bones Radio now," Joe said.

"Yep," Wyatt said. "Just one big happy family."

"Frank and I may need your help," Joe said. "We're pretty new at this. But you've been in this business a long time, right? We may need to ask your advice on a few things."

Wyatt's expression indicated that he wasn't sure whether Joe was putting him on or not. Joe suspected that the announcer was flattered that Joe would ask him for advice.

"Well, sure," Wyatt said, "Any time you've got a question, go ahead and ask. Yeah, it seems as if I've been in this business forever, though it's really only been about ten years."

"You used to work for Ben Harness, didn't you?" Joe asked casually.

Wyatt's eyes narrowed. "How'd you know about that?"

"Was it a secret?" Joe asked innocently. "I guess somebody at WBBX must have mentioned it to me."

"Yeah, I used to work for him," Wyatt said. "Those were the good old days."

100

"Do you still see Ben Harness?" Joe asked.

Wyatt's eyes clouded with suspicion. "What are you driving at, Hardy? What do you want to know about Harness?"

Joe decided that it was time to stop playing games and tell Wyatt the truth. "Frank and I saw you with Harness yesterday. You met him on an island in the middle of Barmet Bay."

"You guys have been following me?" Wyatt asked. "What do you care what I do on my off time?"

"We were just curious," Joe said. "Curious why you were meeting with Ben Harness."

A sly smile crept across Wyatt's lips. "Oh, I got it. You want a cut of the action, don't you?"

"What action?" Joe asked him, a note of false innocence in his voice. "I don't know what you're talking about."

"The payola action," Wyatt said. "Money for airplay. Money for playing Harness's records over Skull and Bones. It isn't legal, but it helps to pay the bills, right?"

"Well," Joe said, "why should *you* get all of it? Isn't there something in it for Frank and me?" Joe hoped that if he played along with Wyatt's illegal plans, the deejay would feel free to trust him.

"You stay out of my territory," Wyatt snapped. "I'm Ben Harness's connection here at Skull and Bones, and the two of you aren't going to get a share of it, understand?"

"Yeah, I understand," Joe said. "So how did you get on Harness's payroll, anyway?"

Wyatt laughed. "I've been on Harness's payroll for years. He started up Harness Records right after I went to WBBX. He got in touch with me immediately, telling me which records to play, sending me a check every month."

"So how did he know you'd moved to Skull and Bones?" Joe asked.

"I called him and told him as soon as I got the job," Wyatt explained. "Believe me, Harness is more likely to pay me every month than this Jolly Roger guy, whoever he is."

"So you don't know who Jolly Roger is, either?" Joe asked casually.

"Nah," Wyatt said. "It's some kind of big secret. But I don't care. I'll get paid one way or the other. Either by Harness or J.R."

"I guess that's one way of looking at it," Joe said.

After Frank's shift ended, the Hardys headed back for shore aboard Steelhart's tug. Once they reached Bayport, they headed straight for WBBX, to fill in Bill Crandall on the latest developments.

But the minute they walked through Crandall's office door, they knew something was wrong.

"Sorry, guys," Crandall said. "I've got bad news."

"What?" Frank asked. "Did Chet mess up on the air again?"

"Chet always messes up on the air," Crandall said. "Not that he's had much of a chance today. Skull and

Bones has been overriding our signal all day, as I'm sure you two know."

"Right," Joe said. "So is that the bad news?"

"The bad news for you two is, you're off the case," Crandall replied. "We're pulling the plug. We don't need your services anymore. You're fired!"

11 Lights Out

"Fired?" Joe shouted. "What are you talking about? We've infiltrated Skull and Bones, we're getting close to finding out who Jolly Roger is and . . . and you're firing us? Why?"

"All right, then," Crandall said. "Who's Jolly Roger?"

"Well, we don't quite know yet," Frank said. "But I'm sure we're on the right track."

"That's not good enough," Crandall said. "Not that it matters. If it were up to me, I'd keep you on the case. But word just came down from Charlie Horwitz. He's giving up, folding the station. He doesn't want you on the case anymore. In fact, there *is* no more case."

Crandall handed Joe a memo from Horwitz, which

said essentially the same thing that Crandall had just said. After skimming it for a few seconds, Joe stuffed it angrily into his shirt pocket.

"He's giving up?" Joe said incredulously. "I don't believe it! How can he give up so easily?"

"Maybe you should ask him," Crandall suggested.

"I think we will," Frank said. "Come on, Joe. Let's pay Horwitz a visit."

Frank and Joe stormed down the hallway and into Charles Horwitz's office. The station owner looked up and smiled as they entered.

"Hello, boys," he said. "I had a feeling I'd be seeing you this afternoon. I gather you've already talked with Bill Crandall."

"Yes, we have," Joe told him. "And he says you've pulled us off the case."

"That's right," Horwitz said. "Because there's no reason to stay on the case. I'm closing down WBBX and declaring bankruptcy."

"But you can't do that," Frank said. "Give us a few more days to catch Jolly Roger, and there won't be any reason to go bankrupt."

"No can do," Horwitz said. "That's just throwing good money after bad. Advertisers are dropping our station like flies. Nobody can hear their ads as long as Skull and Bones is broadcasting. If I get out now, I can cut my losses. I'm fairly well to do, so I'll survive."

"What about Jack Ruiz?" Joe asked. "He's co-owner of the station. How does he feel about what you're doing?"

"Jack has encouraged me to do it," Horwitz said. "I'm even making things easy for him. I'm buying out his half of the station before I fold it. That way he doesn't suffer a loss, and I can take the whole thing as a tax write-off."

Frank and Joe exchanged glances. Should we tell him about our suspicions concerning Ruiz? Joe wondered. Something in his brother's expression told him that it wasn't the right time to bring up the topic.

"Well, it doesn't seem right," Joe said finally. "What about the FCC? They wanted us to keep tracking down Jolly Roger."

"What the FCC wants is to close down Skull and Bones, with the help of the Coast Guard," Horwitz said. "With WBBX closed down, the Coast Guard can go ahead and do the job, instead of worrying about whether this Jolly Roger fellow has some sort of vendetta against us. This will be easier for all concerned, including you boys. You can get back to your own lives now."

"Hey," Joe said. "I was a disc jockey at this station. Now I'm out of a job!"

"That's true," Horwitz said. "So if you apply for a position at any other station in this area, I'll put in a good word for you. Sound fair?"

"Well, I guess so," Joe said. "But I still hope you change your mind about closing down WBBX."

"I'm afraid I won't," Horwitz said. "Sorry about that." He stood up and shook hands with the Hardys, wishing them luck.

106

Frank and Joe left Horwitz's office and wandered, silent and sullen, toward the front door of the station. Finally Joe turned to Frank and said, "Well? Are we going to quit?"

"Are you crazy?" Frank smiled. "Have we *ever* quit a case before it was solved?"

"Never," Joe replied. "And we aren't quitting this one until we find out who Jolly Roger is."

"Right," Frank agreed. "So what is our next plan of action?"

"I think we should check out Ben Harness again," Joe said. "If he's making illegal payments to Keith Wyatt to play his records on the air, then he could be into other illegal things as well. Even if he isn't running Skull and Bones, he may be renting that warehouse down at the docks to whoever is."

"Right," Frank said. "We need to get a look at his files to find out whom he's renting the warehouse to, if anybody."

"But how can we get into his files?" Joe asked. "That receptionist will stop us if we try to get into his office."

"I've got an idea," Frank said. "Come on. Let's get back to the van."

Joe and Frank climbed out of their van in front of the building where Harness Enterprises was located. They were each wearing overalls and carrying toolboxes that they had stored in the van. With Joe in the lead, they entered the lobby of the building.

Joe glanced around, looking at all the walls of the

lobby in turn. "No, it's not here," he said finally. "Let's try the basement."

"And let's be sure to take the stairs," Frank added.

The two brothers entered a door marked Stairs and walked down one floor, stepping into an unfinished basement area. Bare wires and pipes were visible on the ceiling. On one wall was a gray metal door with a handle on it.

"Here it is," Joe said. "The circuit-breaker box." He yanked open the door. Inside were dozens of small switches. Three of them were labeled Harness Enterprises. He carefully threw each switch into the opposite position.

"That should do it," Joe said, turning to his brother. "Now, should we pay a visit to Harness Enterprises?"

"The sooner, the better," Frank said.

They walked up the stairs in case the circuit breakers had affected the elevators. When they reached the first floor of the Harness Enterprises offices, they stepped through the door and into the foyer.

There were no windows in the foyer, and it was so dark that Joe could barely see the receptionist on the other side of the room. She was talking into the phone, shouting at someone on the other end.

"It's a power failure!" she was saying. "Can you get somebody up here right away?"

"Don't worry, ma'am," Joe said, flicking on his flashlight. He kept his face turned slightly downward in the unlikely event that she would recognize him.

"We're electricians. We'll have the problem fixed in a jiffy."

"Oh, thank goodness!" the receptionist exclaimed. "I was at my wit's end. Mr. Harness is in the middle of an important meeting. And there are no windows in the conference room—it's pitch black."

"Just a problem in the wiring, ma'am," Frank said. "If you'll let us into the office area, we'll have the problem taken care of in ten minutes."

"Well," the receptionist said cautiously, "I'm not supposed to let just anybody into the offices of Harness Enterprises."

"We're not just anybody," Joe reminded her. "We're electricians. Without us you'll be in the dark the rest of the afternoon."

"I suppose you're right," she said. "Just go through those doors. I guess you can find the electrical systems. I wouldn't have the slightest idea where to look."

"That's our job, ma'am," Frank said, pushing through the glass door that led into the offices of Harness Enterprises. "We'll be finished in no time at all."

Once they were on the other side of the doors, Joe shined his flashlight left and right, squinting into the darkness. "They must keep their files in some obvious place, right?"

"Right," Frank said. "Look for some large filing cabinets."

"Excuse me?" a voice said nearby. "Did you say something about looking for the files?"

Startled, Joe turned to see a secretary in a small office, seated behind her desk, barely visible in the darkness. "Yes," he said hastily, shining his light into her office. "We think the electrical systems are near your main file cabinets. If you could just show us where those are—"

"Right down the hall there," the secretary said, pointing. "On your left."

"Thank you," Joe said, moving down the hall.

As Frank followed Joe, he glanced into the rooms they passed, making sure that they didn't bump into Harness. Joe made his way down the corridor, using his flashlight to locate the file room. Sure enough, on their left was a large room filled from one end to the other with filing cabinets.

"Oh, great," Frank said. "Where do we begin?"

"I'll check this side and you check that one," Joe told him.

Playing the flashlight beam up and down the file cabinets, Joe read the labels on the front of each drawer. Frank did the same on the other side of the room. "Here are some cabinets labeled Rental Properties," Joe said.

"Okay, check them out," Frank said, moving to Joe's side of the room. "If Harness was telling the truth about renting Bayside Warehouse, it should be in there somewhere."

Joe pulled open the cabinet and started to thumb through a group of files labeled A through C. "Here it is. 'Bayside Warehouse.'" He pulled out the file folder and held it up where Frank could shine his flashlight on it.

"There are only about two hundred papers in that folder," Frank said. "This could take us all night."

"Be patient," Joe said, flipping through the pages. "It shouldn't be buried too deeply. As a matter of fact, I think I've found what we're looking for."

He held up a sheet of paper that bore the legend Rental Agreement and ran his finger down the page. "According to this," Joe said, "Harness is renting the warehouse to something called the Jelly Roll Corporation."

"Jelly Roll?" Frank said. "What kind of name is that for a corporation?"

"Maybe they make jelly rolls," Joe suggested.

"Wait a minute," Frank said. "Jelly Roll . . . Jolly Roger!"

"Jack Ruiz," Joe added. "Just one J.R. after another."

Suddenly the lights came on. "Uh-oh," Frank said. "Somebody must have checked the circuit breakers. We'd better get out of here before somebody gets suspicious."

Joe stuffed the folder back into the drawer and pushed it closed. The Hardys hastily exited the file room and headed for the foyer.

As they passed the receptionist, she said, "That was very quick. Thank you."

"It was nothing, ma'am," Joe said on his way toward the stairway door. "All in a day's work."

The receptionist's eyes narrowed. "Wait a minute," she said. "Don't I recognize you from somewhere?"

"I'm sure you've seen us around the building, ma'am," Frank said, pulling open the door to the stairs.

"And I hope you don't see us again anytime soon," Joe added, hurrying down the stairs after Frank. The Hardys ran out a fire exit on the side of the building and wasted no time jumping in the van and making tracks.

"According to the rental agreement," Joe said as Frank drove the van through the middle of Bayport, "the Jelly Roll Corporation is located at Two-twenty-seven Lembeck Street, right in the center of town."

"Well," Frank said, "this is Lembeck Street. Where's number Two-twenty-seven?"

"It should be right over there," Joe said, pointing at the opposite side of the street.

Frank looked where Joe was pointing. "It looks like an empty lot to me."

"It sure does," Joe said. "There's something awfully funny going on here."

Frank parked the van. The Hardys climbed out and walked toward the lot. There had been a building there at one time, but most of it had been torn down. Part of a wall and the foundation remained. The lot was covered with dirt and debris and construction equipment. There was a large motorized crane with a wrecking ball dangling from the end of it in one corner of the lot.

"Maybe the Jelly Roll Corporation went belly up just as WBBX is about to," Joe suggested.

"And then they tore down the building?" Frank said. "Not likely. I think somebody's pulling a fast one, giving the address of a vacant lot on that rental form."

"Ben Harness?" Joe said.

"Maybe," Frank said. "He could have concocted a fake rental agreement. On the other hand, maybe somebody's pulling a fast one on him."

A mechanical grinding sound suddenly filled the air. Frank looked around, trying to determine where it was coming from.

"What's that noise?" Joe asked.

Frank turned his head. Suddenly he saw where the mechanical sound was coming from: the crane in the front corner of the lot, which was only about twenty feet away from them. It was starting to move, the wrecking ball at the end of it swinging through the air.

And it was swinging straight toward the Hardys!

12 The Vital Clue

"Out of the way!" Frank shouted.

Joe looked up, startled by the sound of Frank's voice, and saw the wrecking ball coming toward him. "Whoa!" he shouted. "Who started *that* thing moving?"

Both Joe and Frank flattened themselves against the ground as the ball swished just over their heads. It took the ball only a few seconds to reach the end of its long arc, then start swinging back toward them again. Whoever was directing the ball seemed to have lowered it a notch this time.

"Move your tail!" Frank shouted. "That thing's going to pulverize everything in its path!"

Sure enough, the ball struck a large block of concrete foundation, smashing it into flying pieces,

114

though the force of the collision didn't slow the ball. Joe threw up one hand to protect his face from the fragments and dived forward to avoid being hit by the ball. Frank did the same.

"There must be somebody in the cab of that crane, making that ball go!" Joe shouted. "We've got to stop them."

"How do we make it to the crane?" Frank said. "That ball's coming back again!"

"Run *toward* the crane when you get out of the path of the ball!" Joe yelled, dodging the ball yet again. "He can't hit us if we get too close to the cab."

Sure enough, as they raced toward the base of the crane, the ball was no longer able to follow them. A dark figure jumped out of the other side of the cab and began to run away.

"There he goes!" Frank shouted. "Let's get him!"

Both Frank and Joe ran after the escaping figure. All they could tell from a distance was that it was a man in a dark jacket, running as fast as he could.

Unfortunately, he had too much of a lead on the Hardys. By the time they reached the next corner, he was nowhere to be seen.

Frank pulled up sharply, bending over with his hands on his knees, trying to catch his breath. "Terrific! We lost him. That may have been Jolly Roger himself."

"Well, he tried to kill us in the empty lot supposedly owned by the Jelly Roll Corporation," Joe said. "Maybe that was Ben Harness."

"Could be," Frank said. "The only way to find out

115

is to pay another visit to Mr. Harness's house—bodyguards or no bodyguards."

This time the Hardys approached Harness's estate from land rather than sea. The long driveway that led toward Harness's mansion was blocked by a metal gate. Next to it was a booth in which a guard sat watching oncoming vehicles.

Frank pulled up to the booth and smiled at the guard. The face that smiled back at him was that of the short-haired bodyguard who had apprehended him on the path the previous evening.

"What are you doing here, kid?" the bodyguard asked. "I thought Mr. Harness told you to get lost."

"We want to talk to Mr. Harness," Frank said. "We've got a few more questions for him."

"Mr. Harness has answered all of the questions he's going to answer for you boys," the man said. "Do us a favor and drive your vehicle back out of here—now!"

Frank sighed and put the van into reverse. But as he was backing up, a black limousine pulled up directly behind him.

"It's Ben Harness," Joe said, looking at the rearview mirror.

Frank braked, and the van squealed to a stop. "Fancy running into you like this," he said under his breath.

The Hardys jumped out of the van and walked back toward Harness's limousine. The driver, who was the other bodyguard from the night before, opened his door and moved menacingly toward the

Hardys. Ben Harness stepped out of the backseat and waved the driver to one side.

"You boys are persistent," Harness said, folding his arms in front of himself. "But I'm not sure why you keep coming around here. Is there something you need from me?"

"Information, Mr. Harness," Frank said. "We've learned that your company rents the Bayside Ware house to something called the Jelly Roll Corporation."

"The name is familiar," Harness said. "So what?"

"So the Jelly Roll Corporation doesn't exist," Joe said. "Its corporate address is an empty lot in the middle of Bayport."

Harness looked astonished. "Doesn't exist? Then how in the world could I be renting to them?"

"That's what we'd like to know," Frank said. "Furthermore, when we went to check out this empty lot, somebody tried to kill us with a wrecking ball."

"Kill you?" Harness said, his eyebrows shooting up. "That's terrible. But I could have told you boys that you'd get in trouble if you poke your noses where they don't belong."

"What we want to know, Mr. Harness," Joe said, "is where you were half an hour ago."

"Are you implying that I might have tried to kill you?" Harness said scornfully. "Half an hour ago I was finishing up a meeting at my office. Which was delayed because of a power failure, I might add."

Frank glanced at Joe. If Harness knew about the

117

power failure, he must have been in his office—though there was the slim chance that he could have followed them to the vacant lot.

"Is there anyone who can vouch for the fact that you were there—and that you didn't leave the meeting early?" Joe asked.

"Only about fifteen top executives from the Kyata Corporation of Japan, who were meeting with me at the time," Harness said. "Do you want their names and phone numbers so that you can verify my alibi?"

"I guess that won't be necessary," Frank said. "We're sorry to have troubled you, Mr. Harness."

"I trust that this will be the last time that you do," Harness asked.

"I sure hope so," Joe said.

"And that's the latest hit by U2," Frank said, pushing a button on the console in front of him. He pulled off his headphones and stood up to put a record away. A slight rolling motion of the S.S. *Marconi* made him brace himself against the wall. Joe steadied himself on the other side of the room and then continued to pace impatiently.

"There must be some kind of clue around here that will tell us who Jolly Roger is," Joe said. "If we don't find something soon, the Coast Guard might shut down Skull and Bones, and Jolly Roger will get away."

"And you'll be out of a job at two different stations," Frank said.

Joe wandered topside again, frustrated at not knowing what to do next. Steelhart's crewmen were still rolling the fuel barrels around. On impulse, Joe followed one of them to the far side of the deck, careful not to be seen.

Instead of taking the barrel into the room where the generator was, however, the crewman punched a hole in the top of the barrel and poured its contents down a hatch, directly into the interior of the ship itself.

What in the world is he doing? Joe wondered. Had the crewman gone mad? The fuel must be highly flammable. Pouring it inside the ship might be a good way to cause the vessel to go up in flames.

Joe scurried away before the crewman could see him, returning to the small cabin where Frank was working. He started to tell Frank what he had seen, but Frank was on the air and waved him away. As Joe waited anxiously for a chance to talk to his brother, he began examining the electronic equipment in the cabin.

It looked a lot like the equipment at WBBX, Joe thought. Some of it was even of the same brand names. But then, he supposed that the equipment at all radio stations looked similar and may even have been made by the same few companies.

When Joe bent over a box of CDs to get a better look at its contents, something fell out of his shirt pocket. He reached down to pick it up and realized that it was the memo from Charles Horwitz that

Crandall had handed him at the station the day before. I must have put on the same shirt this morning that I wore yesterday, Joe thought.

He unfolded the memo and examined it briefly. Then, just as he was about to fold it up again, something caught his eye.

Horwitz's signature.

There was something familiar about it—Joe was sure—though at first he couldn't place what it was. Then a chill passed down his spine. Hurriedly he pulled out his wallet and extracted something he had placed in it two days before—the label from the package that had contained the gas bomb.

He held the memo next to the label. The handwriting on the label matched the signature on the memo exactly.

That could only mean one possible thing, Joe thought.

Charles Horwitz was Jolly Roger!

13 No Way Home

"Frank!" Joe shouted, trembling with excitement. "You've got to look at this!"

"In a minute," Frank said. "I'm about to play another record."

"This is more important than your next record," Joe said insistently, rushing to his brother's side. "I've cracked the case!"

"Huh?" Frank looked up at his brother in bewilderment. "Are you sure you haven't cracked your head?"

"No way," Joe said, slapping the two pieces of paper down on the console in front of Frank. "Look at that handwriting. Horwitz was the one who addressed that gas bomb to Chet."

Frank stared at the two pieces of paper, his eyes

wide. "I don't believe this. You're right! Horwitz has to be our man."

"But why?" Joe said. "What would make him try to sabotage his own station?"

"I don't know," Frank said, "but maybe it has something to do with Jack Ruiz after all. Remember what Horwitz said about buying the station from—"

Suddenly the studio door popped open and Jimmy Collins walked in. Simultaneously Frank and Joe stopped talking at the sight of the station manager.

"Hey, you guys," Collins said. "What happened? I was listening to the station in my office, and everything went silent. The record ended, and you didn't play another one. Is something wrong?"

"Um, I guess I just got distracted." Frank quickly plugged a CD into one of the players and pressed a button. "There you go. Sorry about that. I won't let it happen again."

"You'd better not," Collins said. "Remember, you guys are still on probation here. I haven't decided yet whether I'm keeping you full-time."

"I understand," Frank said. "It's just that we were talking and I lost track of time."

"That's right," Joe said, picking up the two pieces of paper from the console and sticking them in his shirt pocket. "We should be more careful."

"Maybe you two shouldn't be in the studio together," Collins said. "Too distracting."

There was a sound of shouting from outside. Joe recognized it as the sound of Steelhart's crewmen jovially insulting Collins.

122

"What's with those guys?" Joe asked. "Why do they hate everybody involved with this station?"

"They don't hate everybody," Collins said. "Just Jolly Roger. The rest of us just sort of take the flak."

"Why do they hate Jolly Roger?" Frank asked, putting his next CD into one of the players.

"It's apparently something personal between J.R. and Steelhart," Collins said. "I'm not sure, but I think J.R. is blackmailing Steelhart."

"Blackmailing?" Joe asked in surprise.

"Yeah," Collins said. "I don't think Steelhart really wants to rent this ship to J.R., but I think J.R. has some sort of information about Steelhart that could put him in jail. So Steelhart cooperates with J.R. even though he really doesn't want to."

"I thought you said Steelhart was a loony," Frank said. "He sure acts like one."

"Oh, he is," Collins said. "But not so loony that he wants to get locked up in jail. Still, I think one of these days Steelhart is going to cause J.R. a lot of trouble. I just hope I don't get caught in the middle."

"Whoops!" Frank said as the CD neared the end of the track. "I've got to get back to broadcasting."

"Good," Collins said. "I'll get out of here and let you boys do your job."

Collins stepped back out into the hallway, and Frank announced the next song. When he finished, he turned off the microphone and turned to Joe.

"All right," Joe said. "What were we talking about before Collins walked in?"

123

"We were trying to figure why Horwitz would sabotage his own station," Frank said. "Maybe it has something to do with him buying Ruiz's half."

"That sounds good," Joe said. "Do you suppose Horwitz is really planning to declare bankruptcy?"

"Maybe," Frank said. "And maybe not. Maybe that's just a ruse."

"At least we know now why Horwitz wanted us taken off the case," Joe said.

"Yes," Frank said. "And we'd better hope he doesn't know that we're still on the case. Or he might have us removed forcibly."

Joe shuddered. "Right. It's a good thing we didn't tell him that we're still investigating."

"So what should we do now?" Frank asked. "Finish our shifts?"

"We've only got about an hour to go," Joe said. "We might as well, so we won't raise any suspicions. Then we better get back to Bayport as soon as we can and tell somebody what we've learned."

"Who should we tell?" Frank asked. "John Kitchener?"

"I think we should go straight to Bill Crandall," Joe said. "And he can call the FCC."

"Sounds good," Frank said. He hurried through the next half hour of his shift, playing CDs one after another. But suddenly, with only a few more minutes to go, he turned abruptly to his brother. His face was stark white, as though something horrible had occurred. "Uh-oh," he said. "I think I may have made a terrible mistake."

124

"Huh?" Joe said. "What did you do? Play the same record back to back?"

"Worse than that," Frank said. "Remember when you came over here to show me those signatures, and we decided that Horwitz must be Jolly Roger? Remember how I was about to play another CD?"

"Right," Joe said. "And you forgot to play the CD, so Collins came in here to tell us that we were transmitting dead air."

"Yeah," Frank said. "But I don't think we were transmitting dead air."

"What are you talking about?" Joe asked.

"It just occurred to me," Frank said. "I think I'd already opened the microphone when you interrupted me. Everything we said went out over the air!"

Joe's jaw dropped open. "Oh, no! That means that Jimmy Collins must have heard what we said about the case."

"Yeah," Frank said. "Of course, everybody listening to the station heard it, too."

"This is like a good news–bad news joke," Joe said, shaking his head. "The bad news is that the bad guys heard us, the good news is that the good guys may have heard us, too."

"We've got to get out of here," Frank said. "I bet Collins heard us, but he lied about it when he came in here because he didn't want us to know that he'd heard. We would have run away immediately if we knew he heard. He probably called Jolly Roger—Horwitz—right after he left the room!"

"And Horwitz will have to do something about it," Joe said. "Right away." He stood up. "We've got to get off this ship!"

"Maybe we can talk Steelhart into taking us back to shore," Frank said. He pulled another CD out of the box and plugged it into the player. "There's a twenty-minute cut on this CD. If we start playing it now, Collins may not notice that we're gone until we're already halfway back to Bayport." Frank pressed the button, and the CD started to play.

"Good move," Joe said. "Let's get out of here!"

Joe opened the door to the studio quietly and looked out into the hall. Collins was nowhere in sight.

"Let's go," Joe whispered. "It's now or never."

Joe sprinted up the short flight of stairs, just ahead of his brother. He popped open the hatch that led out onto the deck—and came face to face with Jimmy Collins!

"Well, well," Collins said. "What are you two doing up here? I thought the shift was still in progress. Keith Wyatt isn't even here yet."

"We're, uh, just stretching our legs," Frank told him. "I played a really long cut so I'd have time for a break."

"Great idea," Collins said. "That's an old disc jockey trick. Play the longest record that you've got and go eat lunch. Works every time."

"Right," Joe said. "See? We've only been here two days, and already we're old hands."

"So," Frank said, edging away from Collins,

126

"we're just going to walk around the deck for a few minutes."

Collins smiled maliciously. "You're not trying to get away, are you?"

Joe tried to look innocent. "Get away? What in the world are you talking about?"

"You know what I'm talking about," Collins said. "I heard every word of your conversation—the one where you figured out who Jolly Roger is."

"Terrific," Frank said. "Well, Jimmy, consider that if *you* heard it, then everybody in Bayport heard it. Bill Crandall will definitely call the cops, who will be here any minute."

"No such luck," Collins said. "I've got a switch in my office that immediately cuts off the transmitter if something goes over the air that I don't like. The moment I realized what you were talking about, I threw the switch. Nobody out there will have the foggiest idea what you were trying to say."

Joe gulped. "Including Horwitz?"

"I'm afraid I gave Mr. Horwitz a call immediately," Collins said. "I also have a cellular phone in my office. He was *very* interested to hear what you'd found out. In fact, he was shocked to find out that you were working here at the station. From what he told me, you two are also employed by WBBX. Apparently, you never bothered to tell him that you had gotten a job here as well. Just as you never told me what your real names are," Collins said, his black eyes glittering with anger.

"That's right," Frank said. "But it doesn't matter

that you've found that out. You can't stop us from leaving this ship."

"I can't?" Collins said with a laugh. "What do you plan to do, swim? Steelhart isn't back from Bayport yet, and he's the only transportation that you have."

The sound of a motor rose up from the bay. The Hardys looked over the railing to see a small yacht heading straight for the S.S. *Marconi.*

"In the meantime, I have a little surprise for you," Collins said. "A visitor. You're about to meet with Jolly Roger himself!"

14 Disaster at Sea

The yacht pulled up against the ship, and Charles Horwitz dismounted, climbing the ladder up the side of the S.S. *Marconi.* A hulking man followed him.

Horwitz pulled himself over the railing and saw the Hardys. He looked out of place on board, with his expensive black suit and perfectly groomed silver hair.

"Well, hello again, boys," he said. "I hear you've finally cracked the Skull and Bones case. I wanted to be the first to congratulate you."

"Very funny," Frank said. "Now we know why you weren't so anxious to have us crack it."

"True enough," Horwitz said. "Now I think we

should all go down to the studio, where we can have a nice private conversation."

"If it's just the same to you," Joe said, "I'd rather stay out here."

"It's *not* the same to me," Horwitz said. "Pete, can you show the boys a little persuasion?"

"Gladly," said the man. He looked like a professional wrestler in a suit. The dark blue jacket fit tightly over his bulging chest and narrow waist. He had thick red hair and a pug nose that looked as though it had been broken in several fights. He pulled a gun out from behind his jacket and pointed it at the Hardys.

"Now, if you'll just do as I asked," Horwitz said politely.

"I guess that does change things a bit," Frank said. "Let's go back to the studio, Joe."

The Hardys preceded Horwitz and his thug, Pete, back through the hatch, down the stairs, and into the studio, with Collins bringing up the rear. Once inside, Pete took up an unobtrusive position inside the door as the Hardys sat down in the room's two chairs. Horwitz regarded them with an amused look on his face.

"You're quite a pair of detectives, aren't you?" Horwitz said. "If it weren't for that slip with the microphone, you might have succeeded in getting me arrested for all this. But, fortunately, even the Hardy boys make occasional mistakes."

"So far, none of them has been fatal," Joe said.

"That may change," Horwitz said. "In the immediate future."

"What do you plan to do with us?" Frank said. "I don't suppose you could just let us go back to Bayport."

"Not likely," Horwitz said. "You know too much. In fact, I can't let you leave this ship. I know that you've been investigating Skull and Bones all along for Crandall, though I didn't realize you'd already gotten as far as you had. However, it shouldn't be difficult to arrange a small nautical accident, with help from Pete here. Pete helps me out when I need a little extra muscle. It's a pity you couldn't have been introduced sooner."

"That's all right with me," Joe said.

"If you don't mind," Frank said, "I'd like to ask you a few questions about this whole Skull and Bones business."

"Go right ahead," Horwitz said. "I don't suppose there's any rush, though I don't exactly have all night."

"What were you going to gain from this?" Frank asked. "It's your own station that you were sabotaging. Did it have something to do with Jack Ruiz?"

"Good guess," Horwitz said. "Since you boys are the detectives, why don't you tell *me* what I stood to gain?"

"I think I can figure it out," Joe said. "You told us the other day that Jack Ruiz resented your share of the station, but I bet it was really the other way around. You hated to share your profits with Ruiz, didn't you?"

"Quite true," Horwitz said. "Very good!"

"You wanted to buy him out," Frank said, "but you didn't want to pay full price for his share of the station. So you came up with a scheme for making the station look worthless, to get Ruiz to sell out cheap."

"Keep going," Horwitz said.

"You created Skull and Bones to drive away advertisers from WBBX," Joe said, "then offered to buy out Ruiz at rock-bottom rates, as a 'favor' to him."

"Bingo," Horwitz said. "Poor Jack never knew what hit him. He sold out so fast, it made my head spin."

"But what are you going to do with Skull and Bones?" Frank asked. "Now that Ruiz has sold out, Skull and Bones is a liability to you. You can't have it jamming your signal anymore."

"The FCC and the Coast Guard will take care of that," Horwitz said. "The station only needed to broadcast long enough to frighten Ruiz. Now the Coast Guard will close it down, I'll put WBBX back on the air—and the mysterious Jolly Roger will vanish away in the night, never to be heard from again."

"Hold on a minute," Collins said. He had been listening to the conversation from one corner of the room. "You told me that you were going to leave Skull and Bones on the air. I thought this was going to be a full-time job."

"What does it matter, Collins?" Horwitz asked. "You would have worked for me no matter what I told you. You were just a washed-up station manager with no future ahead of you when I found you. You were an idiot to hire these kids, though I suppose I shouldn't have expected any better from you. Now I'm afraid this is the end of the line for you, too. In fact, I'll have to take care of you along with the Hardy brothers. You also know too much."

"Why, you—!" Collins advanced menacingly on Horwitz, but Pete raised his gun. The station manager backed off.

"So were you the one who tossed the grenade in Crandall's window?" Frank asked.

"And tried to electrocute me in the studio?" Joe asked.

"And zapped Chet with the gas bomb?" Frank added.

"Guilty on all counts," Horwitz said. "It was easy enough for me to do all of those things, without anybody becoming suspicious. After all, I was always around the station. Nobody thought it was odd for me to walk into the studio or wander around the building."

"But you tried to make it appear that Ruiz did it, didn't you?" Frank said. "By leaving that package to Chet on Ruiz's desk so he'd have to deliver it."

"And by using the initials J.R. on everything," Joe said.

"That was just a little extra insurance," Horwitz said, "a bit of misdirection in case the famous Hardys

133

found out a little too much. Which, eventually, they did."

"You never really believed we'd get off the case when you asked us to, did you?" Frank asked.

"No, I didn't," Horwitz said. "That's why I had Pete follow you last night and try to get you with that wrecking ball. If you wouldn't stop the investigation when I asked you to, I figured it would be necessary to force you off. Believe me, even if Mr. Collins here hadn't given me a call about your discovery, Pete would have been waiting for you when you got back to shore.

"And now," Horwitz added, "that's just about enough conversation. I'm going to leave you alone with Pete for a few minutes. I'm not interested in the details of how he takes care of you."

"I've got another question," Joe said.

"You're just stalling for time," Horwitz snapped.

"True," Joe said, "but what's a few minutes more?"

"What's the question?"

"What's all this business between you and Steelhart?" Joe asked. "Collins says that Steelhart hates you—something about blackmailing you into cooperating with him. Can you tell us what's going on there?"

Horwitz laughed. "Good old Captain Steelhart. I rented his boat once years ago, when I needed some materials transported for the business I was in at the time. We ended up at each other's throats, because he felt I was trying to rip him off. But I learned that he was using his boat to smuggle illegal goods into this country. I threatened to tell the authorities if he gave me any trouble.

"I looked up Steelhart and told him that he'd better cooperate with me, or I'd have him arrested for smuggling. Of course, I pay him a decent rental fee for this boat, but he and his crew hate my guts. There's nothing he can do about it, though."

"And what about Harness?" Frank asked. "Why were you renting a warehouse from Harness? Is he connected with Skull and Bones, too?"

"Of course not," Horwitz said. "Harness hates me, ever since I drove his station off the air. I just thought it was amusing to rent a warehouse from my old rival—under an assumed name, of course. We used the warehouse to store the fuel and to fix up the S.S. *Marconi* with the radio equipment before she set sail. And I have my sights set on buying that vacant lot from Harness. I'm sure he'll be amused when he sees the new WBBX studio being constructed on property that used to be his."

Suddenly the door to the studio flew open. Keith Wyatt strode in and announced, "Hey, guys! What's happening? I tried to listen to the station on the way over, but you seem to have gone off the air. Is something wrong?"

All at once he noticed the crowd in the tiny studio. "Hey, is this a party or something? Am I invited?"

"Certainly you're invited, Mr. Wyatt," Horwitz said, indicating the gun in Pete's hand. "You're all invited. And I was just on my way out."

135

"I don't get it," Wyatt said. "What's going on?"

"It's a long story," Frank told him. "And somehow I don't think we're going to have time to tell it to you."

"No, you won't," Horwitz said, opening the door. "You won't have much time at all."

Horwitz started to step out into the hallway, but he never made it. From somewhere in the bowels of the ship came the sound of a tremendous explosion. The ship lurched violently sideways, and Horwitz was flung off his feet. Pete spun around and tripped over a chair, the gun flying out of his hand and across the room. There was the sound of gushing water from somewhere down the hallway.

"What in the world?" Collins shouted.

"The ship is blowing up!" Frank yelled. "We're sinking!"

15 Double-Cross at Sea

Pete, Horwitz's thug, lunged for the gun, but Frank got to it before him. "No, you don't," Frank said, snatching the gun from the floor.

"Get out of here, fast!" Collins yelled. "The ship is going down. Everybody better get topside in a hurry."

Collins rushed out the door and up the stairs. Horwitz regained his footing and dashed after him, as did the bodyguard.

"Come on, Frank!" Joe yelled. "We'd better get out of here, too!"

"You don't have to tell me," Frank said as he rushed for the door.

"Would somebody explain what's going on?"

Keith asked, standing bewildered in the middle of the room.

"We'll have plenty of time for that later, Keith," Frank said, grabbing the disc jockey by the shoulder. "Let's get out of here while we can."

Frank followed Joe up the stairs. It wasn't easy, since the ship was now lurching backward at an angle. He grasped the handrails tightly and pulled himself to the top, then reached down to help Keith Wyatt.

"Oh no!" Joe cried suddenly. "It must be the fuel exploding!"

"What fuel?" Frank said.

"I was trying to tell you earlier," Joe said, "but we got sidetracked when we realized that Horwitz was Jolly Roger. I saw Steelhart's men dumping fuel barrels into the hold of the ship."

"Terrific," Frank said as he helped Wyatt up the lurching stairs. "Somebody must have set the fuel on fire. If the fuel's gotten trapped in compartments in the hold, it may blow up a little bit at a time, but pretty soon it'll blow this whole ship apart."

When Frank stepped through the hatch and out onto the deck, he was greeted by an amazing sight.

The S.S. *Marconi* was on fire. Tongues of flame bellowed up from belowdecks, accompanied by thick clouds of greasy smoke. The ship was listing at an angle, obviously sinking, as the explosions continued blasting from below.

In the middle of the ship Captain Steelhart stood

atop a fuel barrel, only partially visible through the billowing smoke. He was waving his arms and shouting, "I've got you now, Horwitz! I've waited years for this! I've got you trapped, and you're going to die like the rat that you are!"

"I was right," Collins said, staring up at Steelhart in amazement. "The old boy's gone completely around the bend. He's blown up his own ship to destroy Horwitz. Steelhart's so crazy he probably didn't even realize he might blow himself up!"

"We've got to find some way back to shore," Frank said, coughing from the smoke. "Other ships ought to notice the explosions, but I don't see any in the vicinity."

"Look!" Joe suddenly exclaimed. "It looks like Horwitz is making a dash for his yacht."

Sure enough, Horwitz had gone over the rail and was now climbing down the ladder, fast. At the bottom he leapt onto Steelhart's tugboat, then onto the deck of his own yacht, which was floating next to it. He then untied the rope that moored his yacht to the *Marconi* and disappeared into the cabin. Seconds later the motor started up and Horwitz's yacht lurched toward Barmet Bay, away from the ship.

Pete leaned against the railing of the *Marconi* and waved a fist at Horwitz. "Hey, come back here!" he shouted. "You can't leave me here!"

"He not only can, he just did," Frank told him as he rushed to the railing. "Looks as if your employer expects you to go down with the ship."

"Give me back my gun," Pete said to Frank.

"What?" Frank told him. "Are you crazy? And let you try to shoot us again?"

"I'm not gonna shoot *you*, dummy," Pete said. "I'm gonna shoot that yacht. That way Horwitz won't be able to get away."

Before Frank had a chance to decide if this was a good idea, Pete grabbed the gun from Frank and pointed it at the side of the yacht. With an expert aim, the man fired three times. For each earsplitting crack of the gun, a tiny hole appeared in the side of the yacht. Seconds later liquid began to pour out of the holes.

"He hit the fuel tanks," Joe said. "Good thinking. That should leave Horwitz stranded in the water. Now we can—"

Joe never finished the sentence. From behind him came the sound of an explosion to end all explosions. He turned to see an immense fireball rise straight out of the other end of the *Marconi*'s deck, only about fifty feet from where he and Frank were standing. The red and orange flames lifted slowly toward the skies, like a miniature version of an atomic explosion.

"I hope that looked worse than it really was," Frank said in awestruck tones.

Even Steelhart paused in his rantings to look up at the fireball. All at once the ship lurched sideways and Steelhart leapt off his barrel. A look of terror crossed his face, as though he had only just realized that he could go down with the ship, too.

"Onto the tugboat!" Steelhart shouted to his crew

as a dense cloud of black smoke rushed over top of the men. He grabbed the railing and started descending the ladder.

"Let's hitch a ride," Joe said, climbing over the railing and heading after Steelhart. "Hey, Captain, how about if you follow Horwitz's yacht for us?"

Steelhart dropped to the deck of the tugboat and looked up at Joe with an icy stare. "I will do my best to catch him, and then I'll cast that demon into his watery grave," Steelhart proclaimed.

"This guy's permanently out to lunch," Joe mumbled as he dropped down onto the tugboat.

Frank jumped onto the deck of the tugboat behind his brother, followed by Steelhart's two crewmen, Pete, Keith Wyatt, and Jimmy Collins. Meanwhile, Horwitz's yacht was still heading for Barmet Bay— but it was losing speed rapidly.

"Horwitz's boat is almost out of gas," Joe said. "We shouldn't have much trouble catching him."

Steelhart revved up the engine of the tugboat as his crewmen untied the mooring rope. They began pulling away from the foundering *Marconi*. Still more explosions were audible from the lower decks of the larger ship, which was now sinking fast.

The tugboat headed straight for Horwitz's yacht. As they pulled alongside, Steelhart slowed the tugboat until they were practically bumping up against the other vessel.

Horwitz was nowhere to be seen. Obviously, Joe thought, he was hiding somewhere in the cabin. One of Steelhart's crewmen grabbed the mooring rope and tied it to the yacht so that Horwitz couldn't get away.

"Let's go!" Joe cried. "I can't wait to get my hands on Horwitz!"

"You and me both," Frank agreed as the brothers leapt from the tugboat onto the deck of the yacht. Apparently everybody either wanted to get their hands on Horwitz or to see what was going to happen, because the Hardys were immediately followed by Steelhart and his crewmen, Pete, Collins, and Wyatt.

"Horwitz must be in here," Joe said, walking up to the door of the cabin. "Do you think he has a gun?"

"He doesn't," Pete said, "but I do. Let me go in first."

"Gladly," Frank said.

Pete threw open the cabin door and stepped inside. Frank and Joe followed. The cabin was quite spacious and luxurious, with padded sofas, polished wood paneling, thick carpeting, and a full set of electronic controls and gear. But there was no sign of Horwitz.

"What happened to him?" Joe asked as the others entered the cabin. "Where else could he be?"

"There's a hatchway here," Pete said, pointing at the floor. "He could have gone down this way."

"Where does that lead?" Frank asked.

"To another hatchway," Pete said, comprehension suddenly dawning on his face, "that leads back out onto the deck!"

"Hey, get back out here!" Collins cried from the door of the cabin. "Horwitz is getting away!"

Frank and Joe rushed back out onto the deck just in time to hear the chugging sound of the tugboat's engine start up again. The tugboat began moving away from them, and standing at its controls was Charles Horwitz. The man smiled smugly at Frank and Joe as they stood trapped on the deck of the disabled yacht!

16 Hitching a Ride with a Fish

"He's pulled a fast one on us!" Joe shouted. "Horwitz came up from below while we were all in the cabin and jumped into the tugboat."

"And he just might get away with it, too," Frank said.

"Oh, no, he won't," Joe said, climbing onto the edge of the yacht as though he were about to dive into the water.

"Hey, what are you doing?" Frank asked. "Horwitz is moving too fast. You can't catch up with him by swimming."

"Want to bet?" Joe answered, launching himself off the side of the yacht in a swan dive.

Joe hit the water cleanly, disappearing below the waves, then bobbed back to the surface seconds later. Inches away from his hands, trailing through the water as the tugboat moved away, was the rope that had been used to moor the tugboat to the yacht. Horwitz had untied it from the yacht. But in his haste he had left it in the water.

Joe grabbed the rope and held on tightly. Within seconds the tugboat was pulling him along in its wake.

Yanking hard on the rope, Joe pulled himself inch by inch toward the tugboat. Horwitz, who had disappeared into the cabin, didn't seem to be aware that he was being followed.

Finally reaching the end of the rope, Joe pulled himself, drenching wet, onto the deck of the tugboat. Apparently hearing Joe clamber his way aboard, Horwitz popped open the door of the cabin and stared at him in astonishment.

"You!" Horwitz cried. "How did you get on this boat?"

"I hitched a ride with a fish," Joe said, staggering to his feet. "I figured it would be awfully boring out here in the middle of Barmet Bay, on a yacht with a hole in its fuel tanks."

"Actually, I suspect it would be quite exciting," Horwitz said, pointing back at the yacht. "Look!"

Against his better judgment, Joe turned and looked at the yacht. Smoke was starting to pour from the lower portions of the vessel, and flames were beginning to lick at its bow. Frank and the others on board the yacht were waving desperately in Joe's direction.

"I took the liberty of setting the yacht on fire before I abandoned it," Horwitz said. "I set the fire in the kitchen, where no one would see it. This way, both the *Marconi* and my yacht will be at the bottom of the ocean by the time the authorities arrive. And there won't be any witnesses left to place me at the scene of the crime."

"I wouldn't bet on it," Joe said, turning around just in time to see Horwitz swinging a small metal anchor in his direction. Joe ducked below the anchor, then punched Horwitz hard in the stomach. The aging station owner collapsed to the deck with a groan.

"You're tough when you've got your hired thug with you," Joe told Horwitz with a sneer, "but you're a real cream puff when you're on your own."

Joe grabbed some rope from the deck and hastily bound Horwitz's hands behind his back. Then he grabbed the controls of the tugboat and headed back for the yacht—just in time for Frank and the others to leap off the deck and onto the tugboat. Within minutes the burning yacht disappeared below the waves.

Almost as if it were imitating the smaller ship, the S.S. *Marconi* chose the same moment to finally give up the ghost. With one final thundering explosion, the *Marconi* seemed to rise up in the water—then it fell back and sank below the waves in less than a minute. The tugboat lurched for several minutes in the wake created by the sinking, then sat still.

"So much for Skull and Bones Radio," Frank said. "Bayport's first and only pirate radio station is now nothing more than a bad memory."

"Which is okay with me," Joe said as Steelhart started up the tugboat and began guiding it back toward Bayport. *Definitely* okay with me."

"It's three minutes after five on a beautiful Friday afternoon. Or is it five minutes after three? Or is this Thursday?" Chet's voice echoed out of the speaker in Bill Crandall's office as Frank and Joe laughed.

"Good old Chet," Joe said. "He never changes."

"Who would want him to?" Frank said. "We love Chet just the way he is."

"It's a dirty job," Joe said, "but somebody has to do it."

"Speaking of dirty jobs," Jack Ruiz said, from where he stood in the door of Crandall's office, "I'd like to thank you boys again for the fabulous job you did getting rid of Skull and Bones Radio. Thanks to you, I won't have to sell my half of this station—and WBBX will be staying on the air."

Joe noticed that he'd never seen Ruiz smiling so much. "Hey," Joe said. "I didn't have any choice. If WBBX had closed down, I would have lost my job."

"Yeah," Frank said, "and I wouldn't have been able to brag about how my brother is the most popular disc jockey in town."

"True," Bill Crandall said, leaning back in his chair, "but what you did was above and beyond the call of duty. I still get shivers when I think about how you guys almost got burned up on the decks of the S.S. *Marconi!*"

"Not to mention on the deck of Horwitz's yacht," Frank added.

"I talked to Kitchener this morning," Bill said. "He says Horwitz will have his broadcasting license revoked. But that's not the worst of it. He'll have to face charges of attempted murder, for one thing. And he'll also have to admit he was involved in commercial bribery, along with Wyatt and Harness."

"You mean for the payola scheme?" Frank asked.

"Right," Crandall said. "I'm sure Wyatt's license will be revoked, too. There will be some extremely stiff fines to pay, also, for anyone involved in the payola. However, it may be difficult to prove— there's no evidence that Harness actually paid Wyatt for playing his records."

"Speaking of evidence," Joe said, "we never found any prints on the gas bomb, but we did trace the handwriting to Horwitz. Were any fingerprints found on the grenade?"

"No," Crandall replied. "But Horwitz confessed to that."

"I still can't believe that Charlie Horwitz was Jolly Roger," Crandall said, shaking his head. "How could he do that to his own radio station? And to you, Jack?"

"Oh, I can believe it," Jack Ruiz said. "We never really liked each other much. Charlie was a nice guy on the surface, but I always had a feeling he was up to no good. Now I know that I was right. But things are working out okay. I'm going to sue Horwitz for *his* half of the station—and it's likely I'll end up sole owner of WBBX."

"That's fine with me," Joe said.

"Tell me this, guys," Ruiz said. "Who was the pirate deejay who first knocked us off the air, before you two started broadcasting on the ship?"

"That was Jimmy Collins," Frank said. "He'll never work in radio again, either."

"No, he won't," Bill added. "And Horwitz's hired man will face assault charges for that trick with the wrecking ball."

"So what's going to happen to Steelhart now?" Frank asked. "Is he going to be arrested for smuggling?"

"Nah," Ruiz said. "The old boy's in no condition to stand trial. I hear he's going to spend some time in a hospital getting his head back together. That was some stunt, blowing up his ship like that."

"Well," Joe said, changing the subject, "I guess I can get my job as an announcer back now, right? I'm ready to start again tomorrow afternoon."

"Um, well, I'm not so sure about that," Crandall said hesitantly. "We might have to wait until another slot opens."

"Huh?" Joe said. "What about the slot that Chet's in? I thought I'd gotten the best ratings that anybody's ever gotten in that slot."

"That's true," Crandall said. "Or it was true."

"What do you mean, it 'was' true?" Joe asked.

"Well, since Chet's been in your slot, the overnight surveys indicate that the ratings have shot up another forty percent," Crandall said.

"Forty percent?" Frank asked. "With *Chet* in the slot?"

"Sure," Ruiz said, an amused look on his face. "We've been getting calls every day since Chet has been on. People love him."

"That's right," Crandall said with a laugh. "They think Chet's the funniest deejay they've ever heard!"

THE HARDY BOYS® SERIES By Franklin W. Dixon

☐ NIGHT OF THE WEREWOLF—#59	70993-3	$3.50	☐ DANGER ON THE DIAMOND—#90	63425-9	$3.99
☐ MYSTERY OF THE SAMURAI SWORD—#60	67302-5	$3.50	☐ SHIELD OF FEAR—#91	66308-9	$3.50
☐ THE PENTAGON SPY—#61	67221-5	$3.50	☐ THE SHADOW KILLERS—#92	66309-7	$3.50
☐ THE APEMAN'S SECRET—#62	69068-X	$3.50	☐ THE SERPENT'S TOOTH MYSTERY—#93	66310-0	$3.50
☐ THE MUMMY CASE—#63	64289-8	$3.99	☐ BREAKDOWN IN AXEBLADE—#94	66311-9	$3.50
☐ MYSTERY OF SMUGGLERS COVE—#64	66229-5	$3.50	☐ DANGER ON THE AIR—#95	66305-4	$3.50
☐ THE STONE IDOL—#65	69402-2	$3.50	☐ WIPEOUT—#96	66306-2	$3.50
☐ THE VANISHING THIEVES—#66	63890-4	$3.50	☐ CAST OF CRIMINALS—#97	66307-0	$3.50
☐ THE OUTLAW'S SILVER—#67	74229-9	$3.50	☐ SPARK OF SUSPICION—#98	66304-6	$3.50
☐ DEADLY CHASE—#68	62477-6	$3.50	☐ DUNGEON OF DOOM—#99	69449-9	$3.50
☐ THE FOUR-HEADED DRAGON—#69	65797-6	$3.50	☐ THE SECRET OF ISLAND TREASURE—#100	69450-2	$3.50
☐ THE INFINITY CLUE—#70	69154-6	$3.50	☐ THE MONEY HUNT—#101	69451-0	$3.50
☐ TRACK OF THE ZOMBIE—#71	62623-X	$3.50	☐ TERMINAL SHOCK—#102	69288-7	$3.50
☐ THE VOODOO PLOT—#72	64287-1	$3.50	☐ THE MILLION-DOLLAR NIGHTMARE—#103	69272-0	$3.99
☐ THE BILLION DOLLAR RANSOM—#73	66228-7	$3.50	☐ TRICKS OF THE TRADE—#104	69273-9	$3.50
☐ TIC-TAC-TERROR—#74	66858-7	$3.50	☐ THE SMOKE SCREEN MYSTERY—#105	69274-7	$3.99
☐ TRAPPED AT SEA—#75	64290-1	$3.50	☐ ATTACK OF THE VIDEO VILLIANS—#106	69275-5	$3.99
☐ GAME PLAN FOR DISASTER—#76	72321-9	$3.50	☐ PANIC ON GULL ISLAND—#107	69276-3	$3.50
☐ THE CRIMSON FLAME—#77	64286-3	$3.50	☐ FEAR ON WHEELS—#108	69277-1	$3.99
☐ CAVE IN—#78	69486-3	$3.50	☐ THE PRIME-TIME CRIME—#109	69278-X	$3.50
☐ SKY SABOTAGE—#79	62625-6	$3.50	☐ THE SECRET OF SIGMA SEVEN—#110	72717-6	$3.50
☐ THE ROARING RIVE MYSTERY—#80	73004-5	$3.50	☐ THREE-RING TERROR—#111	73057-6	$3.50
☐ THE DEMON'S DEN—#81	62622-1	$3.50	☐ THE DEMOLITIO MISSION—#112	73058-4	$3.99
☐ THE BLACKWING PUZZLE—#82	70472-9	$3.50	☐ RADICAL MOVES—#113	73060-6	$3.99
☐ THE SWAMP MONSTER—#83	49727-8	$3.50	☐ THE CASE OF THE COUNTERFEIT CRIMINALS—#114	73061-4	$3.99
☐ REVENGE OF THE DESERT PHANTOM—#84	49729-4	$3.50	☐ SABOTAGE AT SPORTS CITY—#115	73062-2	$3.99
☐ SKYFIRE PUZZLE—#85	67458-7	$3.50	☐ ROCK 'N' ROLL RENEGADES—#116	73063-0	$3.99
☐ THE MYSTERY OF THE SILVER STAR—#86	64374-6	$3.50	☐ THE HARDY BOYS® GHOST STORIES	69133-3	$3.50
☐ PROGRAM FOR DESTRUCTION—#87	64895-0	$3.50			
☐ TRICKY BUSINESS—#88	64973-6	$3.50			
☐ THE SKY BLUE FRAME—#89	64974-4	$3.50			

NANCY DREW® and THE HARDY BOYS® are trademarks of Simon & Schuster, registered in the United States Patent and Trademark Office.

AND DON'T FORGET...NANCY DREW CASEFILES® NOW AVAILABLE IN PAPERBACK.

Simon & Schuster, Mail Order Dept. HB5, 200 Old Tappan Road, Old Tappan, NJ 07675

Please send me copies of the books checked. Please add appropriate local sales tax.

☐ Enclosed full amount per copy with this coupon (Send check or money order only.)
Please be sure to include proper postage and handling:
95¢—first copy
50¢—each additonal copy ordered.

☐ If order is for $10.00 or more, you may charge to one of the following accounts:
☐ Mastercard   ☐ Visa

Name _____ Credit Card No. _____

Address _____

City _____ Card Expiration Date _____

State _____ Zip _____ Signature _____

Books listed are also available at your local bookstore. Prices are subject to change without notice.

HBD-50